Curious

(adjective) – eager to know or learn

Seth King

"The important thing is not to stop questioning. Curiosity has its own reason for existing."

-Albert Einstein

"I know I may be young, but I've got feelings too – and I need to do while I feel like doing. So let me go...and just listen."

-Britney Jean Spears

for my parents.

the ones I was born with
and more importantly
the ones I chose

~

and for J, about whom I wrote this book
thanks for the memories
and for the nights on my trampoline, too...

Inspired by a true story

Prologue

"So how does it feel to have a dick in you for the first time?"

I shift my hips a little and let out some air. To be honest it doesn't exactly feel euphoric or revelatory or any of the other adjectives they use to describe your first time having gay sex – but it doesn't feel bad, *either. It just feels...different.*

"It feels...weird," I pant. "Hold on. Be still. Let me get used to it. You're so big..."

I swivel my hips around to find a better position, and – wow. Something locks in, and suddenly it feels good. Very good. Euphoric and revelatory, maybe. There's one spot in particular, and every time he rubs against it, it sends a crazy ticklish sensation up my core that makes me feel like I'm hurdling through heaven...

Wait, is this a G spot?! Is this what women have been preaching about my whole life? If so, I am officially a believer...

"It feels so good," I moan, my voice sounding somewhat pained. "I almost wish your cock was a little smaller, though."

"Why?"

"Because I think I can feel you all the way in my stomach."

"That's kinda hot. Ready for me to fuck you now?"

"Yeah, just...slow. Please."

And so he starts thrusting into me, filling me, making me crave more of him like nothing I've ever craved before.

"What're you laughing at?" he asks, really giving it to me now, making me moan involuntarily.

"I don't know," I groan. "Isn't it just kind of funny that a few days ago we were friends, and now we're, we'll...doing this..."

"Funny how things change," he says, sinking deeper in me than he ever has before, and activating nerve endings that I didn't even know were there.

"You know what else is funny?" I ask, out of breath. "You said we'd stop being buddies, and start being something

more, the day I find your dick in my ass. I guess that day is here…"

He laughs as he pounds me, giving me a burst of his sweet breath, and for a moment I think of how I even got to this place. Ugh, this was supposed be simple. It was supposed to be easy. A few days of no-strings-attached hookups in paradise with my best friend, who happened to be hot as July – where could we go wrong?

The beginning, actually. The beginning is where we went wrong, and every moment after that was probably a mistake, too. A sublime mistake from heaven and hell. Because the sex turned out to be good *– too good. Explosively, addictively good. And so it led to other things, other curiosities. First I was just curious about his legs, then I was curious about his ass and his abs, now I'm curious about his dreams and his nightmares and his soul and his future, too, in a way I never had before as his "friend." My best friend in the world is now responsible for all of the light in my eyes, and I have no idea what to do about it, because to lose him would take a sledgehammer to my entire existence…*

Suddenly the door of the hotel room flies open. Panic slides into my mind like lightning as I remember that in my haste to get fucked, I forgot to close it all the way – it's all my fault. One horrible moment of dread settles into us, and then with Beau's dick still buried deep inside me, I turn and lock eyes with our visitor as he stops in the entry hallway and stares right at us…

And who is "our visitor," you ask? The very last person in the world who should be here right now. That's *who.*

Nathan Sykes
Earlier That Month

My girlfriend dumped me on a Friday. Five words, one sentence: *I can't do this anymore.* Just like that, like I was a too-old pack of salmon she was throwing out of the freezer. And because salmon rots and stinks, she was doing away with me immediately: she wasn't even giving me the decency of one last weekend. She couldn't even have slept over until Sunday brunch, and then given me the ax on Sunday night? She had to do it on Friday? I mean, really? *A Friday?*

And did I *love* her? I don't know. That wasn't the point. I liked her a lot, to be fair. (I think.) But were we swept away on a glittering road to forever? Maybe not. I still deserved more than a fucking *text message*, though, right? I give her months of my life, and that's what I get in return? A *text*?

Sometimes I feel like nothing I ever do is right. If I come on too strong, I look like a psycho. If I'm too distant, they say I'm not interested and accuse me of cheating. It's like there's this tempo I can't find, this groove I can't slip into – basically dating feels like sitting on one side of a glass partition and expecting to connect with someone. How can we connect when we can't even reach each other?

I spend a few listless hours feeling sorry for myself in a pile of blankets on my bed, cursing the world. Scrolling through my NewsFeed to fill my mind, I stumble across something I can't look away from. And I don't know *why* I can't look away. The story has nothing to do with me.

But I open it and start to read it anyway:

BuzzFeed News
Kate Asher
Staff Writer

The End of Heterosexuality As We Know It?
Citing Online Dating Fatigue and Increasing Cultural Freedom, More Heterosexual Men Than Ever Reportedly Opting for "Straight Sex" With Male Friends

13

But that's when I close out the article. This is just the media being stupid. It has nothing to do with my life, my situation.

I last about two seconds before picking up my phone and reading again:

It is well documented that societal lines are blurring, with today's teens identifying as every shade of the gender and sexual rainbow – or sometimes refusing to identify as anything at all. (In a recent British poll, over one third of millennials described themselves as being bisexual or homosexual.) And today brings a new study showing that these lines that divide us are in danger of disappearing altogether. Nearly twenty percent of the "straight" men anonymously polled in Pew Research's recent study on human sexuality admitted to occasionally having sex with their male friends, despite identifying as heterosexual. Their sex sessions were described as platonic, casual meetings, almost like a shake of hands or a hug between teammates. But stumped sociologists are still investigating what it means on a deeper level.

"Things just aren't what they used to be," says Josh (name changed), a junior attorney in his late twenties living in Brooklyn. "Finding a relationship is harder than ever, since women seem like they want to flit around in these dating apps, and never get serious with anyone. I work like a dog most weeks and weekends, too, just trying to pay my rent and cover my student loan payments. So when I'm single for a long period of time, I'm not afraid to call up a buddy and fool around with him. He'll come over, maybe watch ESPN with me and crack open a few beers, and pretty soon one of us will be on our knees. Or sometimes our backs. It all depends. And then they go home, and I go to sleep, and everything's fine."

"Do you think it makes you gay?" a reporter asks. "How do you relate this to your own personal sexual identity?"

"I don't," said Josh. "And I don't care what it makes me. People don't think in terms of that right now. If I want a physical release, I'm not necessarily going to care about where it comes from."

"What would you call yourself, then?"
"Hmmm. Bored, horny, and curious."

Again, I try to stop reading. Again, I am sucked back in:

According to Dr. Richard Murray, Columbia University sociologist, this trend is a rebellious response to the previous generation's relatively oppressive views on sexuality and gender expression, as well as a side effect of evolving moral standards.

"These kids just don't care," says Dr. Murray. "Many of them describe feelings of being judged or persecuted by the adults in their lives, and they're responding with a total lack of boundaries. The best thing we, as parents and grandparents can do, is simply step aside and learn to live and let live, because these things aren't going to change – and actually, after studying recent trends, I foresee a future dating world where gender could be a factor on par with hair color or personality. Simply another detail..."

I shake my head, roll over, and try to find sleep. Needless to say, it does not find me...something is rolling around in my soul, and I don't really know why, or even what it is...

I've always been straight – I think. But I never cared about what someone was, either. My parents are the staunchest of libertarians, and that's how I was raised – stay out of my life and I'll stay out of yours, too. It always struck me as troubling, America's obsession with getting into someone's mind and their bedrooms. If a kid at school walked in a certain and had too many female friends or listened to the wrong music, rumors would start, and he'd become a moving target. *Who does he like? What are his deepest secrets? What label can we put on him?* So while I'm straight, I'm not rigid in the ways that most of my friends were. But still, I believe that some people are just straight, and some are just gay. I think I'm just...straight, as boring as that sounds.

Aren't I?

On Sunday evening, I stomp my way through the Waldorf-Astoria in Key West, where I've just arrived for a wedding getaway, desperate for solace and trying to sulk in peace. After I find an isolated hot tub/spa in the locker room that seems devoid of any other soul and will hopefully stay that way, I drop my towel, step into the Jacuzzi, and feel my muscles instantly unclench. I didn't even want to come to this stupid wedding, but my friends are all rich, and when planning weddings, the financial situations of their friends are not exactly of utmost importance. And I'm a groomsman, so it's not like I could object…

Anyway, that's how I ended up having to pay eight hundred dollars for my share of this stupid weeklong wedding stay at the Waldorf. (And right now I don't even want to *think* about the irony of having to watch my friend Grant marry his girlfriend Liz on Saturday. We're the same exact age, and he's found his spouse while I'm back to square one all over again. Wedded bliss for everyone except me – *yippee!*)

Just as I start to decompress, the door opens. My pulse speeds up for a second, as I'm naked and could've just been found by some kinky stalker or something, but I go calm again just as quickly when I see the body materializing through the mist.

"Ah, it's just you," I say up at Beau.

"Damn – hoped it would be empty, but this isn't bad, either," he shrugs down at me. He walks over to the bench and drops his towel, but then I do something curious – something very curious. After months and months of having my heart left behind by women, of having them walk away and lose interest and make me feel like shit, I glance at my friend's dick.

And guess what? I don't hate it.

I dart my head away just as he turns to me. "You don't care if I get in, right?"

A shiver of something strange runs through me, then I shrug it off. "Nah. Fuck it, we have the same parts anyway, doesn't make a difference."

"Gotcha."

As he walks down into the water, I try not to notice that his dick is far bigger than mine, and hangs down his leg like an eggplant emoji. Jesus. How did I never notice this?

The steam swirls as he sits across from me. So…I am stuck in a hot tub with a naked dude, and I'm naked, too. This is certainly different, even if we're best friends…

"So what made you ditch everyone and come down here?" he asks casually after he dunks himself to wet his hair. "That game of football was pretty fun."

"I could ask you the same," I tell him as the water drips down his tanned skin. He glances away.

"There were…girl problems, with Megan."

"Ah, I'm sorry," I say, even though I'm not. "What happened?"

He sighs. "She says she's getting older and she thinks I'm not going to commit if I haven't already, and she wants someone she can depend on, and yadda yadda yadda. I basically got dumped."

"Are you serious? I just got dumped, too. That's why I'm here – with vodka."

"Really?"

"Yep, she called me the other day saying she's been feeling insecure, she doesn't know what she wants anymore since she doesn't know what I want out of our future, bla fucking bla. I got the official breakup talk on Friday. I would've told you, but, you know, I guess we both got busy with our relationships…"

"True. We've barely spoken in days," he says after a moment. "That's unusual. And what are the odds we'd get dumped at the same time? I, for one, happen to think we're *great* catches. We just have to find people who agree."

"Ugh. Who knows, but right now I just wanted to sit in this hot tub and forget the fucking world. I brought some vodka in a water bottle, too – that should help. Want some?"

He stares at me, studying me, then finally nods. "Sure. Only after you, though. As you know, I'm only an alcoholic when I'm with good company."

17

I swallow down a revolting shot, then hand it to him. As the vodka warms our bellies we both stare into the bubbling, frothing water, thinking, parsing, analyzing...

"Isn't it funny how people just...cut ties when they don't get what they want from you?" he asks after a minute. "Walk away and act like it was never a thing at all? Sure, I didn't want to get too serious, but why does that mean I didn't *like* her?"

"Do you even want me to get into this?" I ask with a laugh. "Because I will."

He sets his jaw. "Go ahead, then. We never really talked too much about you and...whoever the latest girl was. Fill me in."

I laugh a little, then lean in. "Since you asked...fine. I kind of fucking hate women right now. I'm not gonna lie. I do. I can't believe she dropped me like it didn't matter, like we were never anything, like nothing we did was important to her."

"But aren't you the one who wanted to stay casual?"

"Yes, but only because she was keeping her options open, and I knew it! In all the time we hung out, she never *once* deleted her dating apps."

"Maybe you never gave her a reason to."

"Whatever. I'm so sick of feeling like this, like I don't matter, like nothing helps, like at the end of the day, no matter how many people I'm around, no matter how big the crowd is, no matter how many matches I get on my dating app, like I'm just...."

We say the word at the exact same time.

"*Alone*."

"Wow," I say, and I think I see him shiver.

"Yeah. Megan said she wanted to get serious, too, but I knew she was talking to other people the whole time. I mean, you do have a point – these apps have completely eroded our generation's ability to love each other. Even when I meet a girl at a bar for a Tinder date, she'll have Tinder notifications popping up from other guys right in front of me."

"*Exactly*," I say. "How can we focus on each other when we're always looking over our shoulders for someone better? I was trying to explain this dating scene to my grandma last week and she just didn't understand. She thinks guys still show up at the doorstep, ask the girl's dad for his approval, then take her off for ice cream. I think she'd be shocked to know the truth…"

"That we all fuck each other and then get bored and move on and fuck someone else three days later?" he laughs. "That we can't form anything meaningful because we're all a bunch of commitment-phobes? Yeah, I think she'd be a little confused, too."

"I think that truth-bomb deserves another shot."

"Hear, hear."

Really feeling a little tipsy now, I swallow more of the vodka and then hand it over to him. After another silence – this one more loaded than the first – I clear my throat. "Everything ends the same – we have fun, but we never get deep, and then suddenly it's over. What's the point of it all? Of being here on this earth, alive and alone? At this point, mixing sex and romance just doesn't work. I almost wish I could just…disassociate the two, maybe have sex with someone without any attachments whatsoever. Just…a distraction, even a temporary one."

A long silence passes, then he clears his throat a little. "You do have a point. The relationship part of it all was just getting so hard to handle, especially with all the other shit going on in my life."

I look over. Our eyes meet. And suddenly I cannot deny something is happening here.

Something…odd.

I think of that article I found, but then I banish it from my mind again.

I take a deep breath. For the first time in a *long* time I take the chance to study my best friend, to *really* study him. In a different way. Sure, I've known him forever, but I never really cared about his looks – until now. Until that article made me think about things a little differently…

He's six-foot-two, and his body is long and lean and a little muscular, too. He has the body every guy wants – not too big, but not small at all. He's got short, wavy brown hair and eyes that are somewhere between hazel and light brown, depending on the light. But mostly what you notice about him is the sparkle – he has something nobody else does. He laughs louder and stares more intently and walks with more of a pep than other people do. I've known him since he moved nine houses down the street, back on Fincannon Road, in kindergarten. His house had blue shutters that were too bright, and I remember his parents never collected their newspapers, resulting in a constant soggy pile of paper in the driveway. (Due to over-performance we both skipped the first grade together, solidifying our bond even further.) Before Beau I felt like a mistake in human form – I was too short, too quiet, too this, too that. But he became my partner. He's more outgoing and popular than I ever was, but he was always by my side at the same time – we were a package deal.

But in the last six or eight months, I'll admit that he's had so many girls revolving around him, it kept him from hanging out with me as much – he was simply too busy with the girls.

"Fuck," I say soon, still tense and distracted and frustrated.

"What?"

"Do you really wanna know?"

"Sure."

"It's just...I haven't been laid in *so* long. We were rocky for a while, so we weren't hooking up as much, and then I came on this trip. I'm *really* fucking horny at this point, actually."

He turns away a bit. "Ah. I know what you mean. Megan wouldn't have sex with me for the last two weeks. She said we had to figure out our relationship first."

"Well that sucks."

"Except I didn't get 'sucked' at all..."

My breath catches, but I try not to show my reaction. For some reason I am struck by the face of my cousin, Todd.

Over a drunken game of cards after my great aunt Cathi's funeral last year, he confessed that sometimes when he's really horny, he gets off with his male friends. He said that sometimes they just jack off in the same room to some porn, but sometimes they suck and even finger each other – but he claimed he was straight, and that he was just "using his friends' bodies for pleasure." It sounded like textbook homosexuality to me, but I didn't care anyway, so I didn't think much of it. Now, though, it's certainly more of an issue in my mind. Especially after that article. I'm here for seven days and I'm too exhausted and discouraged to go out and spend multiple nights wooing and meeting and charming girls. I want sex *now*, without trying. Maybe we could work something out…

Or am I being crazy? Did my quarter-bottle of vodka contribute to a random train of thought? Or am I really considering this? And would I even enjoy that?

And what would *Beau* think of this? Would I drive him away, and would he "out" me to everyone and ruin our vacation?

Then again, suddenly I remember that he *did* choose to enter a hot tub naked and alone with another guy…

I pause again. Some of our friends are openly dismissive and condescending about the whole gay issue, some don't care, and a few have voiced support for friends of ours that have come out. Largely it's not really an issue, though – my dad told me that only uneducated people would ever have an aggressive problem with gay people. I can't remember Beau ever really giving a shit, but then again, who really knows?

And then I remember – two summers ago, at Caitlin Ebbert's lake house. Nothing really happened, but then again, *something* did. I walked in on Beau masturbating in a bedroom, and in the split-second between the time I barged in and then turned to leave, at the time I thought I saw a bit of curiosity in his eye – maybe even an invitation to join him. Instead of jumping up or covering himself, he just stared at me, his (large) dick in his hands. It was almost like he was…*offering* himself to me. We never talked about it, and I never mentioned it again.

But what did that moment mean? And why did I just bury it away without any further analysis?

Suddenly the tip of his dick bobs in and out of a pile of bubbles, up at the surface of the water. Then it disappears underwater again. Just as before, the sight of his cock sends a curious jolt down my legs, a jolt I've never felt before. Or *have* I felt it, and I just didn't notice or care because I was too distracted by the women in my life?

"Hey," he says.

"Yeah?"

"Remember Jamie Ross' house?"

My breath hitches – of course I do. At Jamie's sleepover we played Spin the Bottle, but the losers had to jack off together and see who could shoot the furthest while everyone watched. Neither of us got picked, but I watched from next to him as two guys from the soccer team masturbated together across the room.

"Yeah," I say a little nervously. "Wow. Kids are...weird, huh?"

"I guess. But..."

"Yeah?"

"Did you *dislike* it?"

"Um. No. Did you?"

He moves his leg away – only his knee is showing, but I still notice it. "I mean...not really. Honestly it was kind of...exciting."

Whatever the case, this confirms it – I could totally get off with him tonight. With Beau Lindemann. He's thinking about the same thing, and we're both single and drunk and bored...

Maybe I just want to jack it with him, and that's all. Just the thrill of being naked with him could be the thing turning me on – maybe that's it, and I just want another set of eyes on me as I please myself.

His dick appears and disappears in the bubbles again. The skin is smooth and pale and supple. He doesn't notice the little show he's performing, and I don't tell him – I'm enjoying the view too much.

"I have something crazy to say," I tell him soon, after taking one last shot of lukewarm vodka.

"…Yeah?"

"Well. We're both single, and the bride's party isn't even getting here for days. So we don't have access to women for, like, a good while."

"Yeah…"

I inhale, my heart thundering. "Are you sure you want me to say this?"

"Just say it!"

I swallow one more sip of alcohol, then halfway face him again. "You know, it's funny – people are getting more…*open* now."

"Open about…what?"

"Open about…stuff. About sexuality, and all that. You know my cousin Ty in Savannah is super gay, right?"

"Yeah, he's pretty cool."

"And he's living a great life. It's not just him, either. There are all kinds of genders in *Time* magazine, all kinds of sexualities. Maybe you can be something else, if you want. Anything. Or nothing at all. The other day I read a news report about pansexual people. Apparently they don't look for gender in a partner, only personality. And there are friends who hook up, too – guy friends. Pretty modern. Pretty cool…"

He eyes me more intensely, then swigs from my bottle. "Okay…where are you going with this?"

"Who knows," I say, my voice wavering. "All I'm saying is that maybe on this trip I should start thinking about…other things. Maybe sometimes…friction is friction. Sometimes a mouth is a mouth. Sometimes…a hole is a hole…"

A jolt runs down my legs again. There it was – the mention of it. The fruition of our teasing and alluding and dancing around the subject. But what will he say?

A long, agonizing silence stretches between us. Then he laughs and looks away. "I mean…"

"What? What is it?"

His face as red as the flip-flops he was wearing when he came in, he glances away. "*Well*...once, in kindergarten, I got sent to the principal's office for pulling down my pants and showing my dick to a boy named Taylor Perez."

"Oh. Why?"

His eyes glow, then spark. "I don't know. I think I was...well, testing boundaries. Playing around. Being curious."

"Have you ever...done that since? Besides the stuff we've talked about before?"

"I don't know. Maybe."

"*Maybe?*"

He reaches down, and I can't deny it this time – he just touched himself. In front of me.

My body convulses as he continues.

"Fine. I'm only saying this because I'm drunk and we're on vacation in Florida, but...I sucked dick once at Camp Ridgecrest."

"*Sucked dick*?!" I ask with wide eyes. "Wait – our summer camp? Our *Christian* summer camp?"

He nods, smiling wildly. "Remember Walker Ridge, the cabin with the showers in the back room? I dropped to my knees and sucked someone off, for like *maybe* two seconds. Then we got scared."

I look away, then swallow. "And...do you remember what you felt?"

For a moment, only silence. Then he clears his throat a little. "I felt...exhilarated. Dangerous. Thrilled, maybe."

"Wow."

"Yeah. But we were all there for six weeks without any girls in sight, so it wasn't *that* out of the ordinary. Lots of the boys were doing it. Um, have you ever...?"

"No. Not that I can remember."

"*Would* you?"

"I mean, I think it's obvious, considering that I brought this up..."

He doesn't respond. Both of us stare into the water as the air seems to get even hotter and wetter around us. I can't believe we've never talked about any of this explicitly, but then again, I can. What reason did we ever have before now?

"You know what?" I ask soon. "It's weird. I've been thinking."

"About?"

"It's just...sometimes I feel like our lives are planned out for us. Everyone we know is so similar – they go to college, graduate, get married, get a job with some corporation that doesn't give a shit about them. Sometimes I feel like our lives are mapped out at birth, and all we have to do is get from point A to point B. But I don't want that. Sometimes I want to...blur the lines a little."

He blushes, then glances away. "Why are you telling me this?"

"Because, I mean...it's vacation, isn't it? We're in Florida, aren't we?"

He inhales. "Well, sure...and I am single...shit, I guess I *would* give anything for some hot chicks to come suck me off right now..."

I feel something in the atmosphere change – the air shifts, becomes downright electric. This is it – this is the moment I can move in and see where this is going, and see where it might take me. I might hate the taste of dick, and I might become addicted – who really knows?

I scoot a little closer on the underwater bench. It is clear that he is hard now, and his dick is long and fat.

I take a long breath, then clear my throat. "I mean, *I'm* here, aren't I? And I have a mouth, too..."

His eyes meet mine, and I've never been so turned on by anyone before – these eyes I have looked into for years are suddenly dark and hooded and pulsing with unbridled desire. "Are you...are you asking me to *hook up?*"

I laugh, but it sounds beyond fake. Maybe I need to walk this back a little. "Bro. I'm asking you to forget everything you thought you knew. That's all. Forget about the rules. They're changing. The lines are blurring. I was just reading about it, actually. And shit – we're two single dudes. Who cares, anyway?"

He takes a deep, slow breath. "So...what now? We...*do* it?"

I pause, then look down at my hands. "I don't know. How...*big* are you?"

He laughs in a casual way that makes me a little more comfortable. "How would I know? I've never, like, gotten out a ruler or anything. Wanna compare? Like back in the summer camp days?"

My breath catches in my throat. "Um, sure..."

I push myself up on the edge a little. He does the same. And then we do the unthinkable – we clutch ourselves and then study each other's dicks.

Don't get hard, don't get hard, don't get hard...

"Not bad," he says, looking down at me. "You're pretty...thick."

"Well *look* at that thing," I choke. "That would impale me."

"I'm not *that* big. Here, let's see closer."

I scoot towards him a little, my pulse quickening. I angle myself toward him, and he holds himself in his hand, facing me.

"*There* we go..." he says, holding them almost against each other. "Yep, looks like I'm an inch, maybe two inches bigger."

I don't even know what to say. This close to him, it's like the air is radiating, exploding...

"Whoa," he says, looking down at my cock. "You're, um – you're getting hard."

I can feel myself growing, but I turn my head. "No I'm not."

To my horror, I get harder, harder, harder, and there's nothing I can do.

"Uh, yes you are..."

"I am not!"

When I'm practically throbbing, I hide it with my arm.

"*Fuck*," I spit, leaning over, and then my best friend shocks the hell out of me by saying this:

"*I didn't say I disliked it.*"

I look over at him, transported by the need I see in his eyes. The moment is here, and I want this.

"Touch me," I say.

"What? Where?"

"Just touch me anywhere, Beau," I say, more quietly. "I need to feel someone. I need to feel that I'm not sitting here alone."

This really seems to get to him. He sits taller, scoots forward, takes a breath, and then finally puts his hand on my pec.

I press my eyes closed, then open them again. Instantly my skin is warmed to a degree that couldn't just be due to the contact. There was some magic there, too. I felt it.

"How do I feel?" I ask.

"It feels...firm, and warm. Like...a man. And hey, are you *still* getting harder?"

I shrug. "Maybe I am. No comment."

He pulls his hand back, but he doesn't move away. Instead I am the one reaching up now, and lightly I place my finger on his chest. I trace my way from his nipple to his clavicle and then down to his bellybutton. Neither of us are breathing. Then, I pause...

"So," he says, his voice pained.

"I guess it's time to let me touch your dick..."

He doesn't say anything. This is the tensest air I can remember breathing in years.

"I mean, unless you're scared?" I ask. He's hesitant, and I know *this* will reach him. If I ever really wanted him to do something, I'd just accuse him of being chicken. He would run a million miles if it meant proving someone wrong.

Sure enough, he sets his jaw. "No. I'm not scared."

"Yes you are. You're being a wimp. This is just two dudes getting off together. What's the problem?"

"Fuck you," he says, and before I know what is happening, he is leaning forward and taking my hand and slipping it onto his shaft.

"Oh," I say, stunned. "Oh."

"Yep. There's my dick. My fat dick. The dick that's been hanging five feet away from you, your whole life. How is it?"

My body is rocked from head to toe. "Um, you're getting hard, and you're...kinda huge. Like, 'porn star' huge," I say as I clutch his dick, not even believing what is happening.

He picks himself up and fully sits on the edge of the Jacuzzi. Now only his shins and feet are in the water. "*And*? Weren't you going to suck it, so I can prove I'm not afraid?"

My whole body clenches. "Um, okay, just let me get used to it for a second. Give me a little time..."

I lean in and feel around. It's...really big, I can't lie. It's paler than I expected, and it hangs almost halfway down his leg. His balls are large, too. It doesn't repulse me, though. If anything I'm strangely attracted to something that looks like a blind mole rat. Who would've thought that these parts could add up to a whole that was so weirdly enticing?

As I feel around, he leans back and moans. He's really enjoying this, too...

"Okay," I say. "I'm gonna suck now. Don't be afraid to tell me if I do it wrong."

"You won't. God, just suck my dick, Nathan," he laughs. "It's not too complicated."

I take a breath. Lick my lips. Lean forward.

Three...two...one...

Contact.

Beau Lindemann

"Wait," I say just as his tongue hits my skin. My best friend – *my very best friend* – is half-naked against me, begging me to hook up with him. How did this happen? How did we get here? This is one of the most dangerous things I've ever done – he is my brother, and if I lose him, I would live in the dark forever.

But at the same time, why do I suddenly want this so badly?

"Yeah?"

"Hold on."

"Oh, do you need some enticing? Scared again, are we?"

He creeps up and reaches an arm across my shoulder. When did this arm get so...muscled?

"But..." I breathe, and his stubble against my ear makes me hard as granite. "But we played in sandboxes together..."

"And I'd like to play in beds with you now. So?"

I lean away, but he knows I want it. "But we took baths together   as   babies..."

"And now we can take showers together as adults. What changed?"

He leans back down and starts pawing at my dick, which somehow has gotten even harder.

"But...but, we went to a fifth-grade dance in the same limo..."

"And now we can dance together whenever we want. Nothing has changed. Stop."

I take a breath and then sigh. "Fine. Suck me. *Now*."

"Your wish is my command, sir," he smiles, and suddenly it is go time.

"Ahhh, *fuck*," I hear myself moan as he darts forward and slurps up the tip of my dick. Then he starts exploring with his tongue. Okay, maybe he's my best friend, but my intuition was right – he *is* good. Better than Megan, to be honest. She didn't know my body; she didn't know what I liked. Sex with her was like trying to read novels in languages we didn't understand.

But this is…different, already. His mouth is wet and eager and he knows just what to do. And it's so…ticklish. "You sure you haven't done this before?"

"Nope, but I watch a *lot* of porn," he giggles.

I push myself further up the edge of the hot tub. *Thank God I trimmed my hair the other night before I got dumped…*

His eyes like two coals, he looks up at me. "I guess you've got a nice one," he says. "Can't lie."

I don't know what to say. A guy is sucking my dick. Not just any guy – Nathan.

"Get ready," he says, smiling up at me, and for the first time I notice how truly attractive he is – strong jaw, straight nose, tanned and plump skin, thick eyebrows. I know it sounds weird for me to be calling a guy attractive in the first place, since I'm straight – but still, he's a looker. It's almost like the possibility of our hookup is already activating something in me that I didn't know existed…

He leans forward again, but this time he doesn't stop. He twirls his tongue around and around and around, and his stubble against my tip is a new and fascinating feeling. The combination of scratchy/soft is unlike anything I've ever felt, and I kinda love it, to be honest. Then he uses his hand, too, pumping me while his tongue gets to know my dick. Maybe it doesn't matter whose mouth is on me – just that a mouth is on me at all. Lord knows I've had trouble getting regular hookups, with all this girl drama in my life…

"Fuck yeah, dude," I breathe as I reach down and grab his hair, really letting myself get into it. A mouth is a mouth, right? "Just like that…"

He speeds up, and soon I can't push back at all anymore – I am transported by his tongue. Then I forget who is doing this to me at all – all I know is that I want it to continue. I was always very vocal with girls, so that's what happens here, too. "Fuck. Mhmm, suck that dick. Show me what you can do, Nate."

I push his head down a little, and he gags on me.

"Hey," he says, and he looks up at me with my cock in his mouth. "Don't make me choke on the cock before I even know how to suck it," he mumbles.

"Sorry," I say. "And it can't be that hard. Just suck until you taste salty stuff."

"Shut up. Also…"

"What?"

He leans back. "The door into here is glass. What if someone comes in, or walks up and sees?"

"Then I guess they'll have a show to watch," I murmur. "Now get back to work."

"Fine…"

Ever-so-lightly he kisses his way down my shaft, coming to a stop at my balls.

"Fuck," I say with my eyes closed. "That was good. Remember that movement, we might need it later this week."

"So I'm good?"

"Suspiciously good."

"Maybe the thing about girls," he says soon, "is that they don't know the spots. They don't know how good it feels to do…this."

He takes a deep breath and then takes me all the way to the root. I gasp and rock my hips forward. He makes a choking sound and backs up a few inches. "Whoa. You're *huge*. That barely fits inside my throat."

"And you're just realizing this?"

"Sorry, I just wasn't expecting that."

He licks for a few more moments, just sort of feeling his way around, and I am in heaven. Soon I find myself wondering why we never did this before…

"Hey," I say after a minute. "How does it feel, anyway?" I ask as I take my cock and hold it against his face. The awkwardness is fading, and now I'm starting to feel like I'm just hanging with Nate again. I slap it against his cheek for a minute, just to tease him. The look on his face tells me he likes it, though. "To suck a guy, I mean."

"It's…not bad. I could get used to it. How's it for you?" he asks with a flick of his tongue against my shaft.

31

"Fuck," I say. "It feels good. You're even better than Gracie."

"Gracie?"

"My ex from a few months ago, remember?"

"No, there are too many for me to track."

"Oh, well, she was actually a kinky little freak. Now keep on sucking before I beat your ass," I smile at him as I lean back again.

"Yes, sir."

He takes me back in there, rolling the tip of my dick around his mouth as he stares up at me, somewhere between expectantly and nervously. Shit, I still can't get used to this. The way his stubble feels against my skin, the way I can see his hard dick hanging beyond and below his face as he sucks, bobbing at the surface of the water...

Shit. I could get into this. I could really, really get into this...

"Suck my balls," I say, caught by something strange and foreign, and he pauses and looks up at me. That's when it strikes me again – holy shit, my best friend's face is between my legs, and he has my pre-cum on his lips!

"I don't know what you mean."

"Fine, I'll guide your face."

I wrap my hands around his head and gently push him down a little, and his tongue makes contact with my balls. *Ahhhhh, so nice.* Yes, I always did like ball stuff more than dick stuff...

"Fuck, dude," I say. "Yeah, suck on them. Explore around there a little."

In a long, slow motion, he licks me from the base of my balls up almost to my shaft. I lean back, stiffen, and let out a moan.

"What?" he asks.

"Nothing, I'm just trying not to come."

"Already? Damn, should I stop?"

"No. Keep going. I'll take care of you in the morning, if you want."

"Really?"

"Yeah, I mean, why not? You were right – there are no girls here with us yet. But whatever – right now, focus on me. You're supposed to be my bitch, right?" I laugh. "Keep licking."

He returns to the area between my legs and starts licking my fat balls in slow circles. My body goes even stiffer and begins trembling. He even reaches down and starts caressing his own cock, too, making my eyes bulge out of my head. I can't believe that this kid, this guy I spent years playing football with and wrestling in the school's side yard, is now moaning and shaking under me. How do I really feel about it?

I bite my lip and decide I don't really feel *anything* – just aroused.

My body starts to feel all light and airy, and I know I'm about to come.

"Grip my dick," I tell him.

"What?"

"I do it when I'm jacking off. Grip the tip of it when I come. It'll trap the semen for a few seconds and elongate the orgasm."

"Um…"

"Just do it!"

"*Fine*. Gotcha."

I start to twitch and tremble, and he wraps his hands around the head of my cock, sending me over the edge. I come, but it's the longest orgasm of my life – the bubbly, effervescent reaction that flows through my body lasts five, ten, fifteen, twenty seconds. Fuck, this is *hot*.

When I finally look down, his hands are covered in my semen, and his eyes are large and confused.

"What?" I ask as I scoot back. "You've never been covered in come before?"

"No, I'm just…really turned on, and I don't know what that means."

"Oh."

"But it's part of our deal, right?" he asks.

"What deal?"

"Let's just keep doing this, all week," he says. "Exploring. Testing – and tasting – things. We will basically exist to please each other, and we won't even focus on girls. For this week, at least."

"We'll talk about it," I say uneasily.

"Well why wouldn't we? Did it turn you on?"

I look away. "Honestly, yes."

"What does *that* mean?"

For a long moment I just watch the water as it boils and bubbles, staring into it as if searching for meaning in a crystal ball. Then I smile and look down at my best friend again. "I don't really care. All I know for sure is that we're about to have a *really* interesting vacation."

~

Twenty minutes later we're settling into our beds in our shared hotel room. (Who else do you think I'd share with?) Strangely, it doesn't feel awkward at all, really – but then I remember that I'm drunk, thanks to Nate. Of *course* I don't feel awkward. I guess we'll see what happens in the morning when the dust settles and sobriety returns...

As I lay there, he sits up. "Okay. We know a few things now, after that."

"What things?" I ask.

"Well, we know that we like each other's dicks, first of all."

"Ha. I mean...can't deny that." I take a breath and then keep going, pushed on by the vodka. "I liked seeing yours. Don't forget asses, too. The way yours looked when you stepped out of the water was...wow."

"Yeah. We also know we've never done this before."

"With each other, at least."

"Yep. And what I know for *sure* is that...I liked it, and I want it again," he says.

"Same. But..."

"Yeah?" he asks.

"The biggest thing *I* know is that…well, I've known you since we were watching cartoons together, and I have no idea what I'll do if this fucks everything up."

"Good point." He pauses. "Are you afraid more than you're horny, though?"

I wait for fear or shame to come. Nothing does. "Honestly…no. And you?"

"Nope!"

Nate smiles and gets out his notebook, which he writes in every single night before bed. It's like his nightcap – it's the only thing that calms his brain enough to make sleep a possibility. Otherwise he'll toss and turn until dawn. Trust me, after years and years of sleepovers with him, I would know.

"Great," he smiles. "See you in the morning, then. Let's rock this shit."

curious
from the diary of Nathan Sykes

in the silence of the night
I must admit that I
~~touch myself~~
and think of you

and now,
I wonder:

what does it mean
that something long and firm
hangs
where before
I only knew gentle folds?

and what does it mean
that you are strong and hard and solid
where before
I only knew gentle rolls of flesh?

does none of that matter
or does all of it matter?

is everything false
or is nothing true?

all I know is that
right now I am
curious
so, so curious
about *you*

and about what it would mean
if you started to mean more to me
than you do right now

and more importantly...

if you already did mean "more"
all along...

Nathan Sykes

A wave brings me into the light. Then another, the initial *thump* giving way to the general sound of the surging froth. Then a seagull squawks, but it's not a pretty, cinematic *caw* like in the movies – it's more of a blurt, a scream. That finally makes me smile and wake up, and I open my eyes and look over at Beau.

First I remember just a *glimpse* of a memory, something soft and feathery and wet – *fuck*. His dick. I'm remembering his dick. My best friend's dick. That I sucked.

I wait for the shame to wash over me. Fuck, last night was...*weird*. And hot. And weird. To suck my best friend, the person who knows me better than anyone in the world...

But shame doesn't come. Not at all. Instead I just feel...well, kind of horny, actually. Again. It was one of the sexiest things of my life, to be honest. I can't deny that. But does he remember? How wasted was he? He could've been drunk when he came in there, and my vodka sent him into blackout mode. Or he could remember every detail and simply not give a shit. Which is it?

Also, I have to remember that this isn't just a random person. This is *Beau*. Sex complicates things, and to hook up with your best friend is a whole new level of weird. If things get awkward, if they sink too deep or get too serious...I could lose him. I could really lose him.

Still, last night was *fascinating*. Because I can close my eyes at any time and picture everything I know about Beau Lindemann, which is...well, everything. I know what the inside of his apartment looks like, I know how he smells, I know that weird thing he does when he eats where he mixes all his side dishes together. Mashed potatoes and corn? Doesn't matter, they're going into the same corner of his plate. But last night was like opening up a new window and seeing into new compartments of his soul. I never knew he'd been thinking of these things, feeling these things...but then again, *did* I know? It wasn't all *that* surprising. Is something deeper going on here?

Since I have some time to kill – he was always a late sleeper, unlike me – I take out my phone and Google some keywords. Before the day starts I want to research situations like this, read some stories of people who may have found themselves in messes like this one…

I fell in love with my best friend – and he's a guy, one article says in The New Gay Times. I scan the story and then realize…oh, great! They stopped speaking after their hookup, and then it got awkward, and they were never able to really hangout again. How encouraging!

But soon I find a story about two roommates who started fooling around, and in this case, it eventually led to full-on *marriage*. These stories seem to confirm what I thought all along – we're now balancing on a tightrope above a volcano, and our two possibilities are probably either death or heaven. Which one will we reach this week?

As Beau starts to stir, I fully wimp out and leave the room. I rush into the shower to avoid him, where I soak for probably half an hour. This morning we're heading straight into a "bonding" golf session on the resort's course with the other men in the wedding, so there won't be too much time for awkwardness, thankfully. But we do brush shoulders when I'm on the way out of the bathroom.

"Oh, hey," he says groggily. He's already in a towel, too, and I can't deny that my eyes track down to the large, gently curving bulge hanging down his leg. *Damn…*

How is he after last night? Does he remember? Is it going to be weird now? I mean, last night his come was all over me…

"What's up?"

Finally he smiles. "Nothing. Want some coffee? I left all the stuff out. There isn't any creamer in sight, which shouldn't be a problem at all for you, though."

I smile back. Of course he would know that I like my coffee jet-black, and sweeter than a sugarcane field, too. In fact, I don't think there's anything about me he doesn't already know…

Well, aside from what he learned last night, I guess.

I make some coffee as he showers. Then I collapse down onto his bed, sitting next to him as he gets dressed. We've done this a million times, we just kept our underwear on. No towels. But after a second he sits straight up.

"Hey. You know what?"

"What?"

"I was thinking – it was nice to wake up in the same room as you this morning."

My vision blurs a little. "Oh. It was?"

"Yeah. None of my girls would ever sleep over after hookups – they would always say they didn't want to wake up looking ugly, but I think they really just didn't want to be seen doing a walk of shame. But anyway…waking up with you, in this way, was kinda…nice."

I just stare at him. "Um…oh?"

He does this awkward thing with his big arms and turns away, and that's when I notice it – he's hard. And he wants me to notice. He's so hard, actually, his tip is above his towel – and it makes my whole body lurch as I remember how good, how salty, how sexual his come tasted when I got a little in my mouth last night.

But at the same time – am I *really* getting hit on by my best friend?! Is this really happening?

"Oh," I say as I look away from his large, thick dick. "*Oh*. Um, I'm guessing you liked last night, too, then?"

"What *wasn't* to like?" he asks as he stands. He drops his towel to the floor as he heads into the bathroom again, and looks back just to make sure I'm watching, too.

And just for the record, I am.

~

The rest of the day is the weirdest cat-and-mouse game I have ever played. Or are we even playing anything at all? It seems like he's committed himself to the idea, but not *really*. This weird sexual energy dances between us, and I don't think either of us know what do to about it. He doesn't even mention it again, though.

40

Today is our first official day of wedding activities – the bride is the biggest Type A personality in the world, and she wants us all to become close before the ceremony. I suffer through a game of croquet and a photo session overlooking the pool before I can even get close to Beau again. But at least one thing is clear: with all this new energy between us, I think it's safe to say *neither* of us gives a shit about our breakups anymore. I know I don't, at least.

The photo session comes and goes. When we walk through the lobby on the way to a waiting van, I notice how every single head turns at the sight of Beau, and for some reason it makes me somewhat annoyed. He just can't be this hot, this charismatic, this…magical, and then turn away from me again, withhold himself in this way. It's not fair. He was always just…*cool* like that. In every way. I've always battled a constant sense of low-grade anxiety, but Beau was always the down to my up. Just being around him was like being drenched in cool water, actually. He just had that effect.

After a "bonding" trip to a local beach with the other members of the wedding party, we finally head back to the hotel for some food. On any other day this would be my paradise – the cerulean water stretches to the horizon, the palms sway with suntan-lotion-scented breeze, the air is warm and lethargic. But all I can think about is our little…situation. When we're back in the room at last, he catches me looking at him in a mirror.

"Yo, killer," he laughs. "You glaring at me for any specific reason, or are you just feeling homicidal in general?"

"Oh. No reason," I say as I turn away. Then I hear him rustling in his bag – and when I turn back around, he's getting out a jock strap.

He drops his pants, staring directly into my eyes. "Oh," he says so casually I want to punch him, as his big, soft dick hangs there. "I forgot you were here. You won't mind if I put this on, right? I'm headed to the gym."

"The gym? In that?"

"Yeah, it gives me a wedgie, but…I like to feel things deep in there sometimes. Why not?"

41

I am practically gagging as he slides his legs into the jock strap and then turns around, showing me his round, muscular ass…

"Did you wanna come with?" he asks as his muscles flex and un-flex.

I catch my breath. "Oh. Sure. You'll probably need protection, anyway, since the sight of you with those visible underwear lines is going to cause a cougar stampede."

As I slip into my workout clothes I try not to notice how fucking sexy he looks in his barely-there black shirt. I also try not to stare at the way it hugs the curve of his back, and shows off his rippling form underneath…

Shit. We're not even at the gym and I'm sitting here creaming my panties – it's obviously going to be a *long* workout. And he's already parading himself in front of me like a male stripper…

We hit the treadmill for about twenty minutes, but very quickly I notice something bad – his huge dick is flopping all over the place as he runs. The jock strap isn't containing him, and in fact he probably arranged for that. Even the women in the gym are stopping and staring. It makes a twinge of protective jealousy sink into my stomach, but I ignore it, just as I've been ignoring most things lately.

When we finish cardio, I notice he's absolutely drenched in sweat, and his shirt is soaked – so he takes it off. The workout has given a temporary boost to his already crazy body, and I can almost feel the temperature rising in the room. Actually, at this point the women in the gym are practically approaching orgasm, and I'm the same. I cannot get him out of my head, cannot stop thinking of how *full* my mouth felt of him, cannot stop wondering what other parts of him may taste like…

He says that today we should do the bench press to pop out our muscles for the beach tomorrow, and of course I have to go first. We load up forty-fives on each end of the bar, but when I lay out on the bench, there is a new problem – he's spotting me, meaning he has to stand at the rear of the bar and help me lift it off the rack, with his giant dick hanging directly in my face. The dick I sucked last night.

I try to look past it, but it's literally inches from my nose, and through his filmy shorts I can see his veins, his throbbing head, even…wait. Is that some seepage? Is he as horny as I am?

I close my eyes and do my ten reps in the dark. When I stand up again, he gets on the bench – only to reveal his huge cock lying against his leg as he prepares to lift.

"That's it," I say, turning away. "I can't do this."

"Do what?"

I take out my phone and text him instead, motioning for him to check his.

Remember what we talked about last night? I ask, red-faced, half turned-away from him. He frowns as he responds.

Um…yeah?

Well you're gonna need to put that dick of yours away, because it's flopping and bouncing everywhere, and it's SUPER distracting, and I'm gonna have to bring up that deal we made again. Male or female, anyone would be turned on by this, you showboat.

I wait for him to show some emotion – he doesn't. Instead he stares intently down at his phone and types this:

Actually I feel the same.

You do? I ask, wondering whether he's being real or just fucking with me.

Yep. Your ass is looking big and plump in those shorts. I've been horny, too. In fact, we'd might as well take care of this now, so wanna meet me in the locker room showers so we can get off and then get back to our workout?

You're serious? What about your drama of the last day or so?

I watch him roll his eyes as he types his response. **There's no drama, weirdo.**

Really? You barely spoke to me today.

He blushes, pauses, then types again. **That's because I want to be choking on your cock instead. That was part of the deal, wasn't it?**

Every inch of me throbs. Perhaps the whole jock strap thing was just a ruse to get me horny again, and I was just too dumb and insecure to realize it. **Oh fuck, don't play with me. If you're serious, look up at me and nod.**

He finally looks up, smiles, and nods.

Wordlessly I head to the bathroom/locker room, which is empty – does anyone ever come back here? When I swivel into the large, open shower area, he's already turning on a faucet behind me, I guess to steam up the room.

I turn back to him, my whole body aflutter. "This is fine, but what if someone comes in?"

"Did you see one guy in that gym?" he asks.

"Oh. Good point. It was all women – women who were staring at that cock the entire time you were running."

"Shut up." Something sad comes into his eyes.

"Hey, what's wrong?"

"It's just…ugh, I really do want to do this, but…maybe we're being dumb. If I get my heart broken by one more girl, I swear I'll walk off a bridge."

A new sensation rises in me – pity. And concern, too.

I walk over and touch his nipple. "Don't, then. Try something else. Try…me. I'm not a girl."

He licks his bottom lip and then widens his stance. "Okay. You're the one that's about to get it, though. But get on *your* knees first."

"What?"

"Can you suck me off, to get me going? It felt so good last night."

"Really? I thought you were freaked out by it…"

"Um, no, I thought *you* were freaked out by it…"

"Well, I wasn't. So clearly we're good to go!"

I drop down to my knees and get up close to him. Shit – he smells so good right now, so manly and pheramonal. I run my fingers along the band of his shorts, then look up at him one last time and wink.

"Get to sucking!" he orders, and I laugh. Finally I slip a finger into his shorts and pull them down. His big dick bounces out, just like that – it's already ready to go. Fuck. It's even *sexier* in the light, all veiny and thick and fleshy. Instead of foreplay, I just lean forward and take him all the way to the base.

"*Fuuuck,*" he says, gripping me by the head. "Yes, dude, oh, fuck. Yes."

I feel him deep in my throat, pushing against flesh that feels like it's almost at my voice box – and it is the most fulfilling thing I've ever experienced. Shit, if being curious was this hot, why didn't we start messing around when we were teenagers?

I take him again, then get an idea. "Fuck my mouth," I say, my voice low and primitive. "Fuck it like it's a pussy."

His eyes roll back into his head as he thrusts his hips forward, making me gag – but not that much, as I had my tonsils and adenoids removed in the seventh grade. He starts pushing in and out, in and out, and I reach down and jack myself off. But suddenly he pulls out. "Shit, have you done this before?"

"What do you mean?"

"You're not supposed to be able to take a *whole* cock, especially not one this fat."

I blush a little. "Oh, well, I got my tonsils taken out in middle school, if you remember, so I have no gag reflex."

"Oh, yeah, I remember – you couldn't eat for two weeks, during winter break."

"Stop talking and give me cock," I say as I lean in and take him again, overtaken by desire. He thrusts his hips and gives me exactly what I want. The faces he's making as he starts fucking my throat again – shit. This is too much. I reach up and run my fingers over his abs, his pecs, his nipples, as I gag and choke lightly on him. He's getting close, I can feel it in the way he's throbbing, so I stop again.

"What now?"

"Suck *me,*" I say. "I deserve some pleasure, too."

45

"You looked like you were pleased enough when you were choking on my meat…"

"Shut up."

"Seriously, though," he frowns, "maybe I'm not ready for that."

I stick out my bottom lip. "Please?"

He sets his jaw, but his eyes are honest. "I will by tomorrow, I swear. Just give me time. In the meantime, I'm about to jack off all over your face again."

"Fine," I say, opening my mouth.

"Nope, nope – keep it closed, please."

"Why can't I taste it?"

"It's an experiment – I want to know how it looks on a guy's face instead of a girl's. Last night was too dark for me to really see."

"Um, okay…"

Two gaspy minutes later, I stare up at him with his warm liquid oozing down my face. Despite his wishes, a little blob hits the corner of my mouth, and I collect some with my tongue and pause. Again, it tastes so good, so…*manly*, if that makes sense.

"The verdict?" I ask. His bottom lip disappears into his mouth again.

"*Way* hotter on a dude's face. Not even a competition, really. I actually don't know if I want to go back to women anytime soon…"

"Good news, then – you don't have to."

~

An hour later we're being sat down at a late lunch in a fancy but bland waterfront resort restaurant. I'm across from Beau, who keeps looking at me kind of strangely. What does it mean? Is he still just electrified from what we did? For the life of me I still cannot figure this out. The sex thing has introduced a strange new energy between us. Is he "making eyes" at me, or just glaring at me? Before, I knew exactly how to act around him, because he was Beau – one of my oldest friends, guy who knew all my most embarrassing secrets and didn't care, etcetera. He's *always* been hard to read, but it didn't matter because I was comfortable with his mystery. I knew exactly who he was, and what he was to me.

But suddenly I am withdrawn and restless. It just gets worse as the meal goes on, too. I keep thinking I'm sitting incorrectly, because if my posture is bad enough I can look like I have a droopy layer of fat underneath my chin from certain angles. Other times I'm positive my voice is sounding too light and airy, so I keep clearing my throat and trying to go deeper. I've been around Beau a million times – why am I so suddenly self-conscious? He's just…*him*.

We keep meeting eyes again, and then I'll get a mental image of his dick and his ass and his legs and his abs, and I'll blush and look away. He keeps blushing, too, and I already want to do something again. But we can't. We've already been disappearing together frequently enough to potentially raise some eyebrows…

Since dessert is being served in a fancy buffet area, we all eventually take our plates and get in line at one end of a curved table. However, when we're passing an area stacked high with desserts and Danish and pastry, one of our buddies, Lane, makes a comment that sends everything crashing down.

"Nah," he says when the hotel employee asks him if he'd like anything from the pastry display. "I just came over for coffee, so I can drink more later and not get tired." Then he turns to Beau and me. "Only fags would want creampuff shit like this, right? Where's the steak, am I right, you guys?"

Both of us turn red and look away. It is only a split-second comment, but it changes everything about the tone around us. I know Lane doesn't necessarily mean anything *malicious*, and that "faggot" is thrown around all the time in the South, but when you toss around words like that, they can still hurt…

And they do. They derail my whole mood, actually. Sure, messing around in privacy is one thing, but what's going to happen if – or when – we have to face the real world, with our little dalliance still going on behind closed doors? A real world that is apparently so cavalier with its hatred, it throws out slurs at random...

Back at the table, Beau's face falls, his body language instantly shuts down, and he angles his entire body away from me. Great – reality is already intruding on the perfect little hookup I've arranged for myself. Talk about blue balls...

~

Something has changed. Already. Beau barely speaks to me on the way back to the room, and then he swiftly changes in the bathroom and emerges with a bland look on his face. Thanks, Lane – fucking cock block. Ugh.

"What's up?" I ask.

"Nothing at all, dude!" he says breezily. *Dude*, I think to myself. He's already friend-zoning me again. Great.

"Oh...cool."

"Yeah. I was actually just gonna hit up the gym again," he says in a way that in no way, shape, or form, leaves the door open for me to accompany him. I feel my temper pulsing in my ears.

"Oh, nice...well, what about the pact?"

He looks away and coughs. "Yeah...I don't know about that. Maybe it was all crazy, lusty, drunk-y talk."

"Ah. Well, okay then."

"Yeah. Well I'm off."

"Look," I say as he turns, making him pause. "It was just an expression. I don't think Lane knew about us when he used that word."

He looks off at nothing, then clears his throat in a false-sounding way. "Yeah. But...what's gonna happen when he *does* know? How is this going to fit into our lives at all?"

I chew on my inner cheeks. "Um. What happened to living in the moment, Mr. Free Spirit?"

He bites his lower lip, then finally faces me and lets the words explode: "Reality. Reality happened, Nathan."

"What do you mean by-"

But he's already gone.

Beau Lindemann

I stomp my way back to the gym for my second workout of the day, but my thoughts are miles away from anything related to cardio.

So. When I was eight, my mom divorced my dad and got my entire family excommunicated from the Catholic Church. I know it sounds ridiculous now, but at the time it became a huge family drama. Religion was always "her thing," as she had immigrated from Portugal and came from a staunchly Catholic Orthodox family. But that period, when my family literally learned we could not step onto my church's property anymore, changed everything about the way I viewed the world. I'd been such a black-and-white thinker before, a right-or-wrong guy who'd suddenly been shunned by the very force that was supposed to stand for love and acceptance and all that. If Jesus, who was supposed to love me unconditionally, would kick me out of the back door because of something I couldn't control, what did "right and wrong" mean in the first place, anyway? What was up, and what was down, in a world that senseless?

I hit the leg machine and kill the fucking shit out of my calves in an attempt to silence the storm in my head. The comment I overheard today was...not ideal. I thought I could throw caution to the breeze and get off with Nathan, but when the whole world will raise an eyebrow, what's the point? How could I ever relax while looking over my shoulder every other second? How could I live with getting rejected again, like I did back then?

I try to calm myself, and compare this to my experience as a kid. That period was when I learned there really wasn't any true authority in the world, and therefore you had to make your own rules. Did I feel wrong when I did that stuff with Nate last night? No, not at all. It was maybe a little...jarring, but I didn't feel any guilt or anything like that in the slightest. So why did Lane's comment make me want to run and hide, anyway? Why was I listening to him when I'd learned over a decade ago that morality was a sliding scale, instead of the strict set of rules I'd been taught?

As I hit the leg press again I search back for any hints that I was...well, like this. I can't really think of anything besides the usual experimentation that all my male friends took part in, whether they'll admit it or not. And fuck, I can't deny for one second that I'm enjoying what's happening now. Nate's lips on my dick, his sturdy back, the curve of his ass...I like all of it. But do I like guys in general, or do I just like *Nate,* for being *Nate*?

I always just sort of took for face value that I was straight – that was just it. Sure, I can remember being curious many times, and even checking people out at the gym or at a sporting event – but isn't that normal? It's somewhat of a struggle for everyone, isn't it? Everyone craves the same sex sometimes. Everyone is kept up at night by fantasies of their friends. Everyone would sneak to the back of Target as a kid to stare at the sexy guys on the labels of the underwear packages...

Right?

Actually...come to think of it, I've never really heard of anyone *else* being this torn about it. Hmm...

As I hit the treadmill for my cool down, the mental image of Nate's dick gives me a chubby, and I realize: regardless of how my brain feels about it, my body is definitely attracted to him. But there's no way I can change the fact that I am suddenly going crazy over him – nothing will take that away. I never thought this would happen, but I can't deny that just thinking of his penis – *his penis* – is making my own penis throb.

I met Nathan Sykes when we were sleeping in Pull-Ups. He knows my darkest secrets and he's heard me tell the worst jokes I've ever told. He knows me back to front, inside to outside. (And now I guess he knows me top to bottom, too. Hehe.) So if we go for this and make a mistake and do it wrong, we're fucked. Finding new friends just gets harder as you get older, and I know I will never find another Nathan Sykes.

51

But at the same time, I think I might *like* him. In a way that is totally different from before. What do I do about it now that my friends are cracking homophobic jokes and we're all stuck on this tiny little island together?

Basically the question is this: where will our secrets go to hide when Key West becomes too small for us?

Nathan Sykes

Beau disappears and doesn't text me for an hour. I spend the time watching Netflix on my iPad and scribbling in my notebook and texting random friends back home, but something is off. I'm bored and I can't think about anything but his comments from today.

When he returns early in the evening, sweaty and blotchy-faced and kind of beautiful, I turn away.

"Hey," he pants. "Is that really your journal? Damn, I can't believe you still keep that. Every day since…what, like, fifth grade, right?"

"About that long," I say quietly, avoiding his eyes. Still, it's so hard staying mad at him. And yes, I *am* one of the last people on the planet still hand-writing into a paper journal. It just helps me get my thoughts out, since my mind buzzes day and night. Sometimes I'll even have these vivid dreams where I'll start writing in my sleep, and I'll have to get up and write it all down before I can fall asleep again. Writing is just sanity for me, I guess. "Grandma Collins said it was the best way to get my thoughts out, and I started that day and never stopped," I tell him. "I've probably got buckets of pages back home, going back all that time."

"Nice, bro."

I frown. There it is – his "bro" bullshit again. He's rubbing it in, the fact that we're no longer rubbing against each other.

"So," he says, "it was funny, I was trying to do cardio, and I realized this older lady was – *hey* – what's the problem?"

"Nothing."

"Really, don't be a dick. Why are you smirking at me like that?"

I lower my voice and smirk. "Dick is what I want right now, not what I want to *be*."

He looks off at nothing. "It's about *that*?"

"It's about nothing," I say, then I angle myself away. Then I decide to test him. Why not fuck around with him, if he's going to fuck around with me? If he's already abandoned our agreement, that's a pretty shitty move, even as a friend. Friends don't take back promises. It doesn't matter if he promised to fuck me or if he promised to lend me five dollars – you don't just go back on your own word.

So I wrap my arms around my knees and look over at him poutily. "Ugh. You know what? I'm so horny."

"Um. So?"

"So…we made a pact."

"…And? What am I supposed to do about it?"

In my fantasies, I get up close to him and stick my lubed-up finger inside him as he inhales and moans. I finger him harder and harder and harder. His leg muscles clench, his pecs bulge, and he finally blows, squirting all over himself.

But none of that happens in reality. In reality, he's just standing here, and he's pretending like last night never happened. Like he never put himself inside my mouth…

I sit back, trying to pretend I'm not hurt. "What's the deal?" I ask jokingly. "Do you want girls already? Again?"

"Hmmm. Maybe I do," he says a little too casually, and my insides seem to fall a little.

"Oh," I say. "Maybe our little agreement wasn't such a good idea?"

He tears his eyes away again. "Maybe not."

"Ha."

"Why are you so bitter? Jealous, or something?"

"I'm not bitter. I've never been in a better place." I pause, then bound up on my feet. "You know what? Speaking of that, I'm actually heading over to the hotel bar right now. I still like girls, too. And I want one tonight."

"Really?" he asks, looking a little concerned.

"Yep. I'm gonna look for one to hook up with *tonight*."

He turns away, exhales, and finally angles back to me and smiles. "You know what? I was doing the same thing."

"No you weren't."

"Yep! I was!"

"Well…have a great night! Maybe I'll see you there?"

"Maybe so!"

I turn into the bathroom and slam the door so hard, a picture falls off the wall. Jesus Christ – two days in, and we're already at each other's throats. But it also feels strangely erotic, in a way. I don't know whether I want to punch him or get on my knees for him. We are either going to kill each other this week or have the hottest sex of our lives – there seems to be no other options for us.

Ready – set – *go*.

Beau Lindemann

Who the fuck does he think he is? I wonder as I change out of my clothes and put on something more appropriate for late-night. He's going after girls? Fuck that. I can play that game, too. Not that I care, but this is about to be a fight till the end. So whatever we were, whatever agreement we made – it didn't work out. So what? He can't just flash chicks around like this. I will get him back for this…

I find the hotel bar and get down to finding tonight's target. Pretty soon I lock eyes with a girl a few people away – she doesn't send a shiver down my back like Nate is starting to, but she's good enough. She has dark blonde hair and brown eyes, big tits, and legs that could strangle someone. I always liked my women a little on the muscular side, which…

Actually, I'm not even going to think about it. I like what I like. It doesn't mean I'm attracted to masculine-looking people. Right?

Whatever. Suddenly someone appears down the bar that makes the crowd go silent for a moment. It's him. And there is fury in his eyes. But guess what? He's about to get exactly what he signed up for – and then some. If he so obviously doesn't want me anymore, he's going to have to watch me with someone else.

I try to focus, but then Nate does something terrifying. He glares at me, turns to a single girl at the bar, and starts flirting with her.

But guess what? I can play that game, too. I can be just as childish and annoying. So I order a beer and shimmy way down the bar to the blonde, then use my tried-and-true pickup line. "Hey. Have we met?"

She appraises me, then throws her head back in a way that tells me she'd be down for hanging out tonight…and possibly even letting me make her cum. You never know, right?

"*Sure* we have," she says. "Good line, by the way. Now buy me a drink, maybe?"

"Sure I will. What's your name?"

"Birdie, like the animal that flies. My real name's Catherine, but it's an old nickname that stuck."

"Well hello there, Birdie. I'm Beau."

And so it begins. She seems attracted to me, but she's not *entirely* an easy sell, though. She also seems kind of...*bored* with me. She keeps going on and on about her breakup drama, and only after she orders two more drinks does she start looking at me more closely and getting more serious.

"Shit," she says soon after I stretch, accidentally revealing my stomach. "Look at that body. What are you, a model or something?"

"Nah," I say. "Just here on...business."

"What's your business, then? Porn?"

This makes me twitch a little. Fuck. I really do love pussy – nothing Nathan says can change that. The way it smells, the way it feels against my face...at this point, nothing but his cock turns me on more. So what if I'd rather have my face buried in Nathan's ass right now?

Fuck, just thinking about him makes me want to...

Stop that, a voice says. You are friends. You are nothing else. Accept it.

I order shots for us, and soon I really get down to business. When I want something I am an expert at getting it, and before too long I know I've really won her over. Her giggles turn into her hands grabbing at my arms, and that turns into feels on my dick and around my ass. For a moment I close my eyes and wish it was Nate doing those things, but then I shake my head. I can't be thinking like that – this didn't work out for a reason, and now I'm straight again.

So I lean into her neck. "Hey, this place is lame. Wanna head back to my porch, on the ocean? I've got some white wine, and an audio player..."

She puts her hand on the bar. "I don't want to go on your porch. Your bed would be better."

Within minutes I take her back to our room, but we get lost in the maze of the hotel for about ten minutes before we get our bearings. Aside from the Nate thing, I really am enjoying myself – I'm at a five-star resort in Florida, after all, and this girl is about to be a damned good lay.

Finally we find my room. After some flirty kissing, I lay her out on the bed and prepare to distract myself with her vagina – but within seconds something throws me totally off course.

It's Nate's messy suitcase in the corner, and the contents spilling out of it. Nate brings this little photo album everywhere he goes, and of course it's fallen open to show a glimpse of the two of us together when we were barely six. Both of us have chubby little bellies and big clouds of light hair, and we look happier than any two kids ever looked together. It makes something wistful and nostalgic sink into me, and I smile and realize – I don't want this. And I don't want him to hook up with anyone else, either.

I want Nate. I don't want this girl at all.

"I'm sorry," I suddenly say. "I can't do this."

I look down and realize she's already undressed. She stops and looks up at me like I just drove over her foot. "*What?*"

"I'm sorry. I really am. I can't hook up with you. I just…can't."

"*Fuuck*," she finally says. "And here I thought I'd found a substitute for my vibrator and my Tumblr porn…" she adds under her breath. "Guess it's back to my laptop again…"

She starts kicking around, looking for her stuff.

"I'm sorry. Can I walk you out? Do you need an Uber or something? Can I do anything?"

"No, I'm at the hotel. And ugh, what a letdown," she says as she starts to cover herself.

"I know, I'm sorry."

"What's the problem, anyway?" she asks soon, throwing me a vicious side-eye as she pulls on her heels.

"What do you mean?"

"Why can't we do anything? Why did you just shut me down like that? Am I ugly or something?"

"No, not at all. You're beautiful, Bethany."

"Birdie."

"Yes, that. Sorry." I smile and look away as my shoulders fall and a pair of hazel eyes fills my mind. "And the thing is...I think I *might* be falling in love with someone."

~

When she's good and gone, I wrap myself up in the blanket, holding the photo album between my legs.

"Goodnight," I say to nobody, already exhausted with the knowledge that sleep will not be finding me anytime soon...not until *he* returns, at least...

If he returns *at all*...

Nathan Sykes

I start back for the room, but I can't focus – my heart is racing, and I feel fretful and nervous and tense. But what does that mean? What am I so conflicted about? Surely I enjoyed fucking women in the past – I got off every time, and previously I'd never even explored men, besides maybe a few wet dreams and curious glances in a locker room or whatever. What does it say about me that Beau is rewriting my sexual history in only a day?

The thing I'll never tell Beau, the thing that made me argue with the girl I met when we escaped to the pool and made out a little just now, was that I accidentally blurted out Beau's name as soon as her lips hit my neck and she started exploring my skin. Clearly her name wasn't Beau, so...yeah. It didn't end well. Actually, I just cock-blocked myself. And now I'm more confused than I even was before.

I slip back into the room, sighing happily when I see him curled up in his bed. I'm so glad he's alone, so glad he's not banging the guts out of that chick from the bar...

I get in his bed and slide under his sheets, unsure of whether he's fallen asleep or not. But soon his voice pierces the darkness.

"Nate?"

My spirits lift instantly. I place a hand on his shoulder, the shoulder of the person I *really* wanted to be with all night. "Yeah?"

"Remember when we used to sleep on your trampoline together all the time?"

I smile so hard, my cheeks get sore. On cooler nights, we'd wrap up our legs together and fall asleep together in my backyard under a blanket of stars. Perhaps that should've told me something was happening under the surface, even then...

"Yeah. That was special, wasn't it?"

He pauses. "Let's make more of those memories, can we?"

And in that moment, I melt for him. But not in the way a friend melts for another friend, or a mother melts for her baby. I melt for him in a way that tells me he owns more of my heart than I ever thought possible.

"Beau, *of course.*"

"I'm sorry," he says soon, and I repeat it back to him.

"Let's not do that again," I say, and he nods and agrees.

And that's it – no more mentions of tonight allowed.

Before long he lets himself rest against me, touching me more than he ever did on the trampoline, and I feel like I am being caressed for the first time in a million years. He makes warmth flow from my back, up my sides, across my face, and down to my toes. If this is what it feels like to be with him in this way, how will we ever go back?

But soon a dark prospect slides into my mind – the prospect of a world without Beau. Tonight was a near-miss, but it could've been a lot worse. For a moment I see a world without my best friend, a world without our talks that calm and soothe and reassure me, a world without his easy, comfortable silence. A world without all the inside jokes we've accrued over the years, a world without the person who knows me better than my mirror does. What will all of those memories mean if I have no one to remember them with anymore? What will happen if this thing really pushes us apart this week? How will I ever handle that?

When his breathing slows and he lets his whole leg fall against mine, my body is warmed from my legs to my ears, and I am struck by a beautiful and somewhat terrifying thought:

If Beau Lindemann isn't careful, he is going to make me fall for him this week – and that could possibly be the worst thing in the world, too. Because if he doesn't end up reciprocating my feelings, I can already say with certainty that I will be leaving my heart – and my very best friendship in the world – on the sidewalks of Key West.

now or never
from the diary of Nathan Sykes

my feelings for you are
one ecstatic migraine of electric neon

red, yellow, and orange, too
swirling into an acid sunset

threatening everything I hold dear

and at the same time
promising a heaven I've never even
been brave enough
to imagine

baby, this thing is
all or nothing,
do-or-die

now or never

and every moment
I'm just spinning faster
and faster...

but when I stop turning
tell me:
will you be there
to greet me?

or will I be
alone again?

Beau Lindemann

In my dream that night, a routine vision of myself riding in a car on my favorite road is disrupted, and suddenly I am yanked into a *very* bizarre scene. I'm watching myself as I sit in Dr. Kepler's office, our old family therapist, next to my mother – yes, my mother. I can't recall seeing her in a dream in some time, and now here I am, observing us in some fantasy therapy session that never happened. She's crying, and I look embarrassed and annoyed.

That's when Dr. Kepler leans over in those standard-issue therapist glasses, big ones with thick rims, and widens her eyes. "Tell me the problem again?"

"He just can't do this," my mom says, shaking her head in that dramatic way she always used to do. "He knows how religious my sisters are, back home. He can't be like this. He can't choose this. It will be so much easier for him if he chooses women..."

"Ah, yes, *about* that," Dr. Kepler says, and for a split-second I think I catch her throwing a wink at me. Then she smiles. "Tell me, Mrs. Lindemann – when did you 'choose' to make the 'decision' to fall in love with Beau's father?"

My mother gasps, and I reach out and touch her cheek. But before I can make contact with her skin, I am suddenly awake.

I look over at Nate and banish the dream from my mind. It's sometime after dawn, and the light is *perfect*. I leer at his body – his nearly shoulder-length dark blonde hair, his liquid-y eyes under those eyelids, his thick shoulders and torso that is somehow thin and muscled at the same time, his fat ass, his large legs...

Shit – setting aside the drama from yesterday, he really *is* a handsome dude. I can appreciate that. Even sober. More handsome than I ever noticed, and I'm noticing it more and more every day. He's about six feet tall, with long golden hair and darker facial hair. He's thin but toned, with a happy trail disappearing down into that space between his legs that I've been admiring so much lately…

In his sleep he paws at his dick a little, and it makes me want to jump out of my skin. Soon it gives me an idea. Hey, I'm horny *now*, so why not have some fun with his body while he wakes up, just to make up for all that stressful drama of last night? That was part of our pact – we were to be of use to each other. Why can't I slurp him up right now? He's supposed to essentially be my cum dumpster, right? So *what* if I'm wanting him a little earlier than I should…

I lean down, uncover his dick, and find that he's at half-mast. It's just resting against is leg, and it's seeping a clear liquid that makes me lurch a little inside. He even smells musky and male. Fuck, this sight *really* turns me on, even though I can't believe it…

I lean down and lightly kiss the tip. He's definitely seeping, probably a little from a wet dream. Shit, this tastes so good…like man and sex and muscle…

He yawns in his sleep and unfurls his body. I am taken aback again by his long, thick legs, muscular towards his ass and leaner down to his ankles. You can see tendons and muscles moving right under his skin, and damn, he's so pale up near his ass and dick that you can see his brownish pubes. Oh, those pubes, I could get used to that sight…

"Hey?" he asks, and I sit up and gasp – he's awake.

"Oh," I say. "Hi."

"What are you *doing*?"

I swallow my pride and decide to just throw it out there. "Well. I kinda wanted to wake you up with a blow job, as part of the pact, or whatever. Is that cool?"

"I mean…if you *insist*…"

"Yeah, yeah, I know it's just *so* torturous," I smile shyly. "I just woke up horny, and – yeah. Get ready."

I lean closer, closer, closer…

"Wait," he says, making me stop. "Before we, um…let's make some ground rules."

"Rules?"

"Yeah, just like they do on the football field. No games without guidelines. I don't want to fuck this up – I said that before, and I really meant it."

"Can't we do that later?" I ask after a moment. "I'm kind of turned on by what's happening in your dick area right now."

"And what's that?"

"Here, taste it."

I can't believe what I'm doing, but I reach down, get some of his liquid on my finger, and then rub it slowly across his lip. He licks it, then pauses.

"Wow," he says, his eyes burning. "Tastes like…salt. And alcohol. Guess we've been drinking a little too much…"

"Now my turn. Okay?"

He swallows, then nods. "Okay."

My tongue gets closer, closer…

"Oh wait," he says, "um…*one* more thing."

"Yes?"

"The thing is, I only come in my girlfriends' mouths, or else I can't get off. I just like how it feels."

"*Fine*, I'll let you come in mine."

"You sure?"

"It's whatever," I shrug. "I get come all over me, all the time, when I jack off. We make the same semen, right? We're both just guys…"

He leans back again with his legs open, propped up on his elbows. For a moment I just stare at him – God, I've never studied a male body like this, but I love it. I'd bet that any woman would pay money to look at this body right now, but the view is *all mine*. Combined with his cleft chin and his playful eyes, it's something anyone would pay to see. I guess there's a reason he cycles through girls like most people cycle through pairs of underwear, even if he thinks it's because there's something wrong with him and everyone dumps him…

Finally I take his dick in my hand. It's not giant, but it's fat, and his balls are much bigger than mine. Shit, I could really get used to these things…

"You ready, or are we just gonna lay here all day?" he asks.

"Oh, yep, I guess..."

I move to his dick and kiss the tip. I have to pause to keep myself from having a surreal, *oh-shit-what-is-going-on?* moment. This is no more wrong or right than if I were kissing a vagina, and I have to remember that. Best friends notwithstanding...

Then I lick him from his tip to his balls, and I find that a rush goes over me when I hit the balls. Damn – I really like these things. I take one into my mouth as I start to jack his dick – it tastes sweaty and male and amazing. Maybe I really am fully bisexual? Who knows – right now all I want is to taste his come, and try it out.

"Touch my nipple," he says. I do it for a minute, and soon I feel more comfortable. I rub him from his pec down to his abs, which are smooth and hairless and defined, then down to his waist – this is the biggest difference yet in the women I've been with, because where a woman's waist is soft and fleshy, his is harder than a bone. He widens his legs as I run my hand down his leg and feel his bulging calf muscles – I can tell he does a *lot* of squats...

Then I just do it – I make full contact with his tip, then take him all the way to the base, meaning I've given my first official blow job – and truth be told, I fucking love it. *Love* it. He's so thick I have to immediately spit him out, but then I do it again, savoring his salty taste this time. It's...different, but not in a bad way.

"Oh fuck...oh fuck," he breathes, and it is a bit jarring to hear my friend talking like this, I can't lie. But not jarring enough to stop. "Beau...yes, suck that cock..."

I take him deep, once, twice, three times. His cock makes a squishy sound against the back of my throat that makes me giggle a few times. I have to remember not to use my teeth, but soon I've found a rhythm. I suck him faster, faster, faster...

He's going to come quickly – I can tell. He tugs my hair hard one last time and then suddenly he is twitching all over.

He groans, goes still, and soon his dick is spurting something down my throat. I can't believe I am seeing my best friend during his most intimate of all moments – an orgasm – but then again, I can. It just feels…natural, somehow.

We each just pant for a minute, and I think he's just as surprised as I am. Then he looks down, still breathing erratically. "Wait, where's my come?"

"Oh, I, um…swallowed it."

"What?"

"Yeah. Couldn't help myself. Easy cleanup."

"Well…what do I taste like?"

"Like…bread, and beer, and salt," I say.

"Is that bad?"

"Not really. Just…*new*."

Our eyes lock, and something zaps me down to the core. Then he tears his eyes away and curses.

"What?" I ask as he takes out his phone.

"It's Lane, wonderful Lane, telling us we're already late for some wedding thing. Guess we'd better get going. *Yay!*"

Nathan Sykes

Before I know it, we're back on the beach. The games we have to play with the other wedding party members are just as boring and uncomfortable as yesterday's activities. As soon as the cocktail hour arrives, Beau and I grab some free drinks from the bar and then get out of there. We've got some sex sessions to figure out...

It was my idea, really, to make our little pact official. So that afternoon we sit on the porch and finally draft up a Key West Constitution. That's right, no more playing around – if we're going to do this thing, we've got to actually do it right. We're messing around with some delicate shit, here – the closest friendship we have in the world, actually – and we've got to go about it correctly. Last night proved that.

"First, no love," he says, and I pause. "I mean, *obviously*. But that would just be...weird."

I study his face. Is that regret I see moving into his eyes?

"I know this sounds like something out of a bad movie or something," he continues, "but...don't fall in love with me, and I won't fall in love with you. Not that we're in any danger of that happening, but...yeah. Neither of us needs that right now. Last night was dramatic enough."

I roll my eyes, but my stomach is falling at the same time. "Trust me, love is a four-letter word to me right now," I say as darkly as I can. "There's no chance of *that* happening."

"Well...*good*."

I pause, then lick my lips. It's a little awkward at first, to be sitting here talking about sex with the best friend you're about to have it with, but that evaporates quickly as our glasses empty again and again. Soon we're drunk and laughing and having a grand old time. I always attached a little more emotion to sex, so I demand a few things that take some negotiating, and he has a few sticking points, too. But soon the list is complete.

68

I set my iPad on the table and read it one last time. I'm an English major probably going into law school, so I'm a little proud of how professional it ends up looking:

The Rules of Key West
by Nathan and Beau
(hereby referred to as The Parties)

1. **First of all, the parties are to serve as each other's sex toys, nothing more, nothing less. This is simply a sexual agreement between friends.**
2. **If one party is horny, the other party must agree to a sexual release, unless serious outside circumstances interfere.**
3. **Protection must be used if requested by the other party.**
4. **No public hookups.**
5. **If one party seeks outside sexual pleasure from another party, the other party should be notified, but is not to interfere.**
6. **Kissing on the mouth is only allowed if explicitly agreed between both parties beforehand.**
7. **No romantic feelings (e.g. 'falling in love') are allowed, under any circumstance. Period.**
8. **See article seven again. Seriously.**

And so it is official: from that point onward, we are each other's sex objects. I exist to please him, and he exists to please me. It's that simple, and until further notice, I don't have to give a shit about girls, or girl problems, or girl *anything*. I've got a big dick at my disposal, and I'm going to get full use out of it.

And it really does turn out that way. We just don't think about anything anymore. I serve him, and he serves me. We hit the gym again that evening for a boozy weightlifting session, except this time we only make it ten minutes before he's begging me to follow him into the bathroom. It seems that the framework of the agreement has freed him already. There's an elderly man in the showers, so we head into the steam room and turn up the steam before I gobble up his dick and don't stop pumping his shaft until he's squirting down my throat.

"Wait," I say before we leave. "I want to come, too."

He knows he has to agree now, so he exhales. "Okay. Come on my face, then."

"Why?"

"Why not? I really liked it – it was so warm and salty and stuff…and I want to feel it in a different way now…"

"Okay, you're getting weird. Just let me blow this load."

"Your wish, my command…"

He kneels under me, reaches up, and massages my nipples while I jack off. Soon I am moaning and he is kissing my balls, and *boom* – a white liquid is all over his cheeks. I rub it around with the tip of my dick just to elongate the moment, and he doesn't object. Damn, he is so beautiful…

"That was easy," I say soon, to nobody in particular, as we head back down the hallway.

"It was. You know what? It's cool not to have to worry about taking a girl out to dinner, entertaining her or dealing with any of the other stuff that comes along with sex."

"Yeah. But…"

"But what?"

"You know, what do you think it means that both of us have had the same issues connecting with women?"

He shivers a little. "I don't know, Dr. Phil, but right now I'm not too concerned. Relax. We're in paradise. Let's just have some fun, and get some dick, too…"

~

As the trip rolls on, we go around together like best friends, but use each other's dicks and bodies like lovers. It's pretty much the perfect balance of heart and penis, and the best thing is that I don't have to worry about getting rejected afterward, or waking up to a text detailing all the different ways I wasn't good enough.

When we wake the next morning, we're so both bashful about our bad breath and stinky armpits that we simply tangle up our legs and jack off together, spurting onto our newly tanned chests at the same exact moment in a reverie of moans and sighs and *"oh, fucks."*

Later, I drag him into a bathroom at lunch to suck on his nipples, but then I end up sucking his dick and swallowing the resulting liquid – and all of it is perfect.

Something deeper is happening, too. I need him more with every touch, I crave him more with every lick, I even smile brighter every time he brings up an old inside joke or mentions an old story from the olden days. It feels too delicate to fuck with, like a Faberge egg balanced on the edge of my knee, so I don't question it. But still we continue to have the hottest and most interesting hookups of my life, and each one intensifies.

They go like this:

- In the evening we're all supposed to meet by the pool, but I can't stop glancing at his arms and his thick legs in his short little bathing suit. Finally he takes the hint and motions for me to go to the bathroom, where he meets me in a stall, drops to his knees, and services me until I bust in his mouth. We return to the group noticeably relaxed, but nobody says anything.

- The next day there's a volleyball match, and it's too much for me – watching his lean, muscled body darting here and there, glistening in the sun, getting covered in sand…our eyes meet again, and this time he's the one who takes the initiative.

  "You don't have a gag reflex, right?" he asks when we rush back to the room.

  "Nope, why?"

  "Because I want to fuck your throat. Like the other day, but more intense."

  "What?"

"I saw it in a porno – here, just lay on your back on the bed, with your head out over the edge."

I do as I'm told, and he slides himself down my throat – and from this angle, I can take *all* of him. Every last inch, actually. I reach around and grip the back of his firm legs as he thrusts in and out, huffing and puffing, fucking my throat deep. When he finally busts down the back of my throat, I choke on the amount of semen he produces.

"Jesus. Are you sure you're not a blue whale?" I ask afterward. "That was probably a gallon of come..."

"I mean, at this stage, *anything* is possible."

And these are only a few instances. By the time that night arrives, I have had four orgasms in one day, slipped in between our other activities.

I am also starting to notice certain things I've never cared to notice before, too. Why does everyone stand up whenever Beau walks into the room? Why does he always have the perfect joke to tell at the perfect moment? Why do women look at him like he invented the sun? What is the magic of this kid, and how can I bottle some of it for myself?

There are other things, too, just between the two of us. The way he caresses my hand when I ask him to help me button a shirt, the way our eyes sort of get stuck in each other's when we glance at each other from across a pool or a table, the way he got really worried when I disappeared underwater for a minute or two. I'm noticing so many things, but most of all, I'm noticing his smile.

Because his smile could save cities. So many people aren't really happy deep down where it counts, and it shows in their faces – when they smile, it doesn't reach their eyes. But when Beau Lindemann smiles, it radiates all the way to his eyes, and then kind of bleeds into *my* soul, too. Something is happening here, blooming right out in the open in front of our friends, and I'm starting to wonder if I am really the only one dancing in all of this new energy...

the fire
from the diary of Nathan Sykes

summer is enveloping us
rolling us into her bosom
taking us away
into lands we never knew before

and tell me
because I want to know:

when my eyes got stuck in yours at the pool today
did you feel it?

and when my heart twitched when you kissed my neck in
the shower
did yours twitch, too?

because baby
I am *in flames* for you
and I'm starting to wonder
if you even really feel any warmth in you at all...

Beau Lindemann

Fuck. I'll admit it – things are happening. And things are…changing, too. Slowly, sure, but still, they're changing. Every hookup is hotter, and every time I catch myself making eye contact with him, it's harder to look away. And soon…

Soon I feel myself wondering a few things, like: when did Nathan's eyes get so hazel? Some eyes are just hazel, but his are *hazel*, like a glass of scotch lit from behind by a roaring fire. Who allowed this to happen? And why did I never notice any of this before?

We always had such a comfortable dynamic that sometimes we'd not even really speak that much – I'd meet him at a bar, he'd tell me with one look that he'd had a terrible day and needed a drink, and we'd scroll away on our phones for a few drinks while we just enjoyed each other's company. But now it's like I can't stop talking. I chat and chat and chat, and once I even get into the situation with my mom – but then I pause and stop myself. I know way too many people who use their wrecked-up pasts to justify their current issues and excuse how they're messes or disasters, and I had such a knee-jerk reaction against coming off like that, I stopped talking about her. Permanently. In fact, I have not uttered a word about her in four years…and yet today I wanted to just blurt it out, just like that…

Anyway, Nathan is starting to feel less like Regular Nathan and more like…well, someone else. Someone new. Someone bright…

I'm enjoying the pact, but is it normal for friends to feel these things? What is he to me now?

"So have any girls contacted you this week?" he asks me after I meet him in the room that night. We're both laid out in bed – the same bed – and the fact that my leg is against his leg is not phasing me at all. "Any snaps, texts, Facebook messages?"

"Oh, I actually…well, I forgot about that. I wasn't even paying attention. Something else came up that demanded *more* of my attention…"

"Ha," he says. "Speaking of that, I was thinking…we need to adjust the pact."

"Okay?"

He swallows. "Yeah. The thing is…I like touching you too much, so *this* is now included in what we can do." He rests his leg over my crotch, then grabs me and rubs my calf.

"I'm fine with that," I smile. Then I reach over and start massaging *his* arm, too. "But I'm adding my own rules. This, too. This is now allowed."

"Fuck buddies who caress each other," he smiles after a minute. "I have to say, this is a new one for me."

"Hey," I laugh, "we already know we're gonna get laid in the end, so who cares?"

He gets a little sad then. "Yeah. Right."

"What is it?"

"Nothing, nothing at all. Hey, turn on *SportsCenter*, I want to see where Templeton went in the trade."

I groan and reach for the remote. "Fine, fine…"

But something strange happens that night: we don't let go of each other. In fact, I fall asleep in his embrace, like we're old married people or something. Who are these people we are becoming? And more importantly, why do I love it so much? Are we already losing sight of the rules we made for each other? Because if we don't have real, true guidelines here, things could go seriously off the rails…

Or maybe, just maybe, they already are.

Nathan Sykes

At lunch the next afternoon, we're all greeting the groom's family, who just touched down in a private jet from Raleigh. His mom, blonde and pale and icy, is making the rounds when she gives me a kiss and then asks me if I've fallen in love.

"*What?*" I ask, almost spitting out my wine.

"You're positively *glowing*, honey. What's her name?" she asks with surprisingly dark, shrewd eyes.

"Hey," says Lane in that bellicose voice of his. "Listen to this. He's been running off with Lindemann every chance he gets, maybe they're double dating some island chicks, and they don't wanna share the love?"

"I'm pretty single," I say to end the conversation – but I know she doesn't believe me.

I turn my glare to Lane. His name is actually Lane Bryant, a fact that nobody ever lets him forget. He comes off as a parody of every bad Southern stereotype rolled into one, except he's *real*: he's got a beer belly that can't be contained by his starched suits and bow ties, his skin is constantly ruddy from his diet of liquor and golf course sunlight, and he's almost always slapping someone on the back and saying something obnoxious (and quite possibly offensive).

Today, the server is being pulled in ten different directions by our demanding and drunken crowd as they order elaborate drinks and scream and yell and shout at each other. Of course, Lane is loudest. Ugh, what a bunch of pushy assholes. I'm halfway considering handing my server a twenty-dollar bill for the hell of it when I see Lane call her over – but he doesn't even speak to her, he *whistles* at her. My blood pressure spikes as she comes over. Lane rests his hand on her arm in a weird, possessive manner that she did not invite in any way. And when she finally escapes, he calls her "sweetie" in his loud, boisterous Charleston accent, like she was a little girl asking her grandfather for a Popsicle. Is *this* how women are treated every day? Because if so, I'm almost glad I was born with a penis...

Beau and I head back through the lobby after lunch, both rolling our eyes at the insane behavior at the meal. He draws all kinds of looks and stares, and I roll my eyes. We're not even dating and yet I'm sick of this already. How would anyone deal with the self-esteem hit that being around him would bring? You're always reminded that he's the star, and you're not. Or maybe he just makes *me* inoperably insecure for some reason?

"God," I say soon, when we're alone.

"What?"

"After certain things Lane kept saying, I'd be afraid you'd get freaked out and call off the pact. He's just so...*hetero*."

"*Duuuude*," he laughs. "At this point, you couldn't keep your dick away from me if you locked it in a cage. That thing you did to my balls yesterday...sheesh."

I try not to blush. "That sounds painful, actually. Dick in a cage?"

"You have no idea – that's why you just need to give it to me whenever I want it."

"Beau?" I ask, when we're changing into our workout clothes. "What do you like about hanging out with me?"

"You're...funny," he says soon, like he's thinking about it for the first time. "In a morbid way. And you see things differently – you have a weird insight into things." He pauses. "Hey, um...speaking of that, what do you like about being with *me*?"

"Well...your body is good, for one." He slaps me lightly on the arm. "Hey! Wasn't done yet. You're always so...even-keeled, and it makes *me* feel calmer, too. I can never freak out around you, because you keep me down low. And obviously, you know everything about me and you never ran for the hills, so that helps, too."

His eyes twinkle for a minute, then he looks away. "Well, I'm glad. Let's go work out and tease the women in the gym with our slutty muscle shirts!"

"Sounds like a plan to me."

The text comes well after the workout, and just after Beau falls asleep cold next to me. He always *was* a good sleeper, much better than me, and I was always jealous about it. There aren't many hells quite like staring at your dark ceiling for three hours while you pray for sleep to come and for your brain to turn off and stop torturing you...

Hey, my friend Trevor says. **Just thought I had an obligation to show you this...**

At first I do not believe the picture he has attached. It's a screen shot of the girl who just dumped me, messaging Trevor on some dating app. The worst app of all, too – the app everyone knows is just for quick, cheap hookups. *Really?* We've been single for what – *days*, and she's already sitting here messaging my *friends*? And she knew Trevor was my friend, too – we've all three hung out together!

Then I read the actual messages, and they are even worse.

Nope, she says in one, when Trevor asks her if she's attached. **Totally single, and have been for a long time. That's why I'm on here, looking for someone, lolol!**

This makes my blood boil. Really? She won't even give me the dignity of naming me? She's already erased our entire history? *Really*?!

First it makes me shiver with something I can't pinpoint, then it makes me angry. Very angry. Stupid liar. She dumped me days ago, and she's already wiped us from her memory.

But then I remember...I'm doing the same thing, too. Just not on an app...

In real life.

And when I think of Beau, suddenly this doesn't even matter anymore. He's like human Xanax. All the emotion just fades away as I look over at Beau, my Beau, who is hotter and smarter and generally more awesome than any of the losers involved in the situation I am fretting over. Why would I lose sleep over a faucet when I have Niagara Falls right next to me?

And so I *don't* lose any sleep. I snuggle up against Beau's back, wrap an arm around him, and sink peacefully into the darkness within minutes.

~

Before I know it I am being awoken by Beau reaching for my cock, which is fat and wet at the tip. It must be ten or eleven in the morning, which I hate, because sleeping in also means wasting half of your whole day. After a minute of letting him paw around, though, I push him off.

"Hey," I say, sitting up groggily. "New rules. Can we do something besides hook up?"

He pauses. "What do you mean?"

"I mean, I almost..."

"What?"

"I almost miss our friendship, that's all. Trust me, I love the hookups, but what happened to doing normal stuff, too? I'm starting to feel a little...used."

He sets his jaw, insistent about something. "You know what? Sure. Wanna kayak?"

"Kayak?"

"Yeah. We have a card for a free rental, and I'm craving some sun..."

"Sure. Good idea. I'll follow you, I guess."

We stop by the rental shack, and soon we are drifting out into the sea in a two-seater kayak, since they didn't have anything else due to the lingering spring break crowds. It's a brilliant blue day, the kind of day people write books about, and after we slice through the tiny, greenish-white waves, we are pushing out into the flat calm of the wide open ocean. It all works together to relax me more than I have been in months, maybe years. When did I become so high-strung, anyway?

"What are you thinking about, weirdo?" I ask soon, since Beau's eyes are miles away.

"Sorry. Just...my mom, actually. I always miss her when, you know, like...big things are happening, I guess."

Well, *this* is unexpected. And I didn't even know I was *a big thing*. "Oh. Wanna talk about it?"

Beau hesitates. We have never really spoken about the death of his mother, soon after his parents' divorce. It's probably the *only* thing we've never spoken about, minus the time he told me about finding her body, right after the funeral. I understood that he needed his own time to shut down and *break* down, too – there was nothing I could say that would make it any better, or change it. His mom was dead in the ground, and I just had to step aside and let him deal with it.

I tried in the beginning, of course, but when doors go unopened and texts go unreturned, you eventually get the picture. So we let it go. But I know the basics. His parents were always much older – when they got married, his dad was over sixty and his mom was in her thirties. So everyone assumed Beau's dad, who was in a wheelchair by the time Beau was in high school, might go at any time. So it was a total shock when his *mom*, a healthy, tennis-playing, gardening-loving brunette, filed for divorce and then just died out of nowhere, of a massive hemorrhagic stroke. Turned out so she was so stressed from taking care of her husband for so many years, her body just…quit on her one day. She thought she was getting a whole new life with her divorce – that never happened. Beau was the one who found her, actually. To my knowledge, I am the only one he has ever shared the story with, and I have never repeated it to anyone. But what I remember most is the haunting detail that their cat, Little, was napping atop her chest when he found her, and refused to leave even when the paramedics showed up and tried to shoo her away.

"It was a nightmare," Beau finally says, his eyes on the horizon. I try not to notice his golden biceps in the Florida sun, but I can't ignore them. Even in a moment like this. "Just a fucking nightmare. There's nothing else to say. Every moment of it sucked."

His nostrils flare. I watch and wait.

"It's like…there's a piece of me that's gone forever now, and there's nothing I can do about it," he continues. "And the worst thing is that she was healthy, she was happy.

Everyone said 'oh, it's such a blessing that Jesus took her without suffering,' but she was, like, *fifty years old* – that is *not* a blessing. We spoke on the phone that very morning – we got into a fight, actually. I was in a shitty mood, and I was totally cold and dismissive. So was she. I never saw her or said a word to her again. Alive, at least."

"I don't know what to say," I finally tell him. "Sorry wouldn't do anything."

"I know," he says. "And I never forgot you. You were the only one who treated me like a normal human in the period after that."

"What do you mean?"

"Death is like a scarlet letter on your family's door," he sighs. "Everyone suddenly treats you like a helpless infant, or goes out of their way to ignore you because they don't know what to say. But *you* were the only person who made it known that you were there, and then stepped aside until I was ready. You treated me like I was still...*me*. I'll always remember that."

"Wow. I had...no idea."

"You were still right, though. What you said once about how you couldn't help. Nothing changes it. Nothing makes it better. It's like knowing you're locked in a bad dream, but being totally unable to wake up."

"Is it any better now?"

"Time dulls your feelings, but the feelings themselves never change," he says soon. "It's just...fury, black and huge. The best you can hope for is to forget about it for a day or two. But you will always remember it again. There will always be a void, and you'll always notice. And now, on some level...I'm afraid of everyone else leaving, too. Why wouldn't they? If the one person who was supposed to be there for me – if *she* left, why wouldn't everyone else leave, too? My life had no rules or order anymore. For many reasons. I couldn't even go to church..."

"Yeah. I remember. Stupid hypocrites."

He swallows. "So. Maybe that's why I'm so distant from people. Love triggers that same fear I felt at my mom's funeral – that fear of being left there, of being the last person on Earth…so I avoided it altogether."

"I will always be here," I say quietly as the water laps at the sides of the kayak. "As a friend, as a brother, as a…*whatever*. Even after you don't want me. I'll be here, annoying you. You know that."

His eyes meet mine. I jump a little. "That's the problem," he almost whispers. "Sometimes I'm afraid I might never want you gone."

My breath catches. "But that doesn't sound like a problem at all…"

He just stares at the horizon. I am not even in the water, but I am still drowning.

"You know what's weird?" he asks soon. "I've never talked about this in-depth before. With anyone. Not even my therapist."

"Maybe you should start letting things out a little more. It's good for you."

"I'll try..."

I just stare into the waves for a while.

"Hey," I ask. "Do you ever ask yourself *why* you're even living the life you're living, in the first place?"

"In what way?"

"Like, I wonder…how much of you was born, and how much was created?"

"I see your point."

"Yeah, I just…more and more I realize how overbearing the South can be on people, especially with guys like Lane. He comes off like a factory product – I doubt he's ever had an original thought in his mind, and instead it's just a constant loop of whiskey and catcalls."

"Sounds about right."

"Yeah. So considering all that, maybe I'm not…*me*. Maybe I'm not…*this*. Maybe I don't even know *who* I am. Maybe I'm just an amalgamation of everyone I've ever met before. You might be grieving, but at least you know who you are. I don't even have an idea."

"Jesus. What's bringing on all this?"

"Don't you wonder sometimes? Especially...*lately*?"

"Fine – of course," he says soon. "Sometimes I feel like I'm just waking up, and everything before this was a nap. But when I look around...what am I going to be, if I'm not *me*?"

I just let the question hang.

"I guess that's what adulthood is supposed to be, isn't it?" I ask eventually. "Answering that question..."

After that we spend twenty minutes talking – about our hopes, our fears, our hobbies, the things that keep us up at night, the things that broke us and rebuilt us. It's the best chat session we've had in years – I feel closer to him than ever. Shit, even if the whole sex thing falls away, I'm still so thankful for our friendship.

He pauses soon. "So...I'm guessing this isn't the first time you've ever been attracted to a dude?" he asks out of nowhere.

"Um. How'd you know?"

"Just a hunch."

"I can't believe we never talked about it."

"I can. Just think of Genaro..."

I groan. Genaro was a member of our fraternity at the College of Charleston who quietly "came out" during freshman year – and then was promptly black-listed. He disappeared, and because he was different, nobody missed him, or even really mentioned it. Including us.

"Actually," he says, "my dad knew."

"What?" I ask as a long stratus cloud blocks the sun.

"Yep. Wow, I'd totally forgotten about this! He found me watching gay porn in middle school. Walked right into the room when I was about to...you know...finish off."

"What? You said you were always totally straight!"

"Once again, I said I was *curious*, obviously."

"Curious..."

"Curious," he repeats. "After that, a switch turned off. He didn't look at me when he spoke, he didn't even acknowledge me when I walked into the room. Our relationship was dead a long time before he actually died."

"*God.* And you think it was because of the porn?"

"I know it was. We were fine before that. He used to be...well, my dad. And then he wasn't anymore."

I can't imagine any of his pain. He didn't even get to find closure with his own dad before he died, too, five years ago. Just like his mom.

"I would never think any less of you for that," I say eventually.

"I know you wouldn't. You're getting dick out of the equation now."

I laugh and splash him.

"I'm so glad we came down here," I tell him. "This is exactly what I needed. And the sex isn't bad, either."

He laughs, too, and we just listen to the birds and the sea. Driven by something I can't name, I put my hand closer to his. He inches his closer, too, then pulls it away again.

"We can't do this," he spits out.

"Why not?"

"Because people could be on the shore, watching us.

"And? We're just touching. And we can't live in fear of that, anyway."

"Nate, get real. It would change *everything*, it would make people talk before we're ready to answer...there are real risks here."

A wave of fear hits me, but I try to push it away. "Stop. With *those* abs, people were going to talk about you, anyway. Trust me."

I slam the paddle into the water and soak him. His mouth drops, and he does the same. Soon we're splashing and laughing and whooping up a sea of foam, and when I get up to push him, he does the same – and we crash into the sea together in a heap of limbs. After we surface, I am struck for a second by his beauty – his hair is perfect in the salty water, his eyes are blazing and radiating heat, his skin is getting darker by the hour. They catch me totally off guard, the butterflies, and soon I start feeling like I am soaring, gliding over the sea, and *that's* when I realize that my best friend has totally just made me woozy.

Well, then...

We just stare at each other for a second there, out in the blue-green ocean, against the edge of the kayak. If you're going to be young and falling for someone, why not do it in the Keys? This is like something out of a novel.

"You're weirdly...*beautiful*," he says, as I feel myself start to melt. "That sounds so strange, but...you are. It's almost genderless. You're beautiful in the way girls are, but at the same time you're totally masculine. I can't explain it."

"You're striking," I say soon. "That's what you are. You're striking looking. Haven't you ever noticed it?"

"Noticed what?"

"When you walk into a restaurant, forks stop in midair. People go silent. They're struck by you."

"Stop. No they're not."

"You're really oblivious to it? I thought you knew, and just didn't care. Seriously, going around with you is a spectacle."

"Aw, stop."

A large wave suddenly comes out of nowhere, and we both duck. When I come up for air, I curse – he's gone. Fuck, where is he? Did he hit his head?

"I'm in here," I hear a muffled voice say. "Under the boat."

I dunk under the water, feel around, and then resurface when I am under the overturned hull of the kayak. The blue plastic over us is lending a beautiful blue-ish glow to his face, and instantly I feel my skin get all chilly and prickly.

"Kiss me, Nathan," he says, very quietly.

"What?"

"I'm turned on by you, and I want you to kiss me."

"Um. That was absolutely not discussed in the rules of our pact...that *you* insisted on, by the way..."

"So what? Fuck the pact. We're in the water now – let's go with the flow."

"Okay. You make the first move, though."

A war wages in his eyes. Will he do it? Or will he run?

Finally he leans in and touches his lips against mine for the very first time, but what follows is not a kiss. It is something that warms and thrills me from my toenails to my chest. It is a symphony, a song, a film from the heyday of black-and-white Hollywood…

In short, it's better than any kiss I've ever shared with any girl. Ever.

He freezes, then pulls his head away, his eyes hooded but confused. "That was…"

"Amazing, I know," I say as a shiver takes flight down my back. "Yikes."

He bites his lip and thinks, then nods and seems to decide on something.

"What's wrong? You're not hesitating again, right?"

"Fuck no," he smiles. "In fact, come back to the room with me."

"Why?"

"Because you gave me the worst case of blue balls of my life the other night during our fight, and you owe me – *big* time."

"*How* big?"

His smirk could light a fuse – it is that hot. "Well, I didn't measure you, but I'd say about six-and-a-half inches. *That* big."

Beau Lindemann

My whole body races as we return the kayak and Nate follows me back to the room, our little sanctuary. Once the door is locked, we breathe more easily.

"Should I?" he asks, fingering his bathing suit. Even though we've done this several times, it's still nerve-wracking every hookup – we still don't know our ways around each other yet.

I nod, then hold my breath…

I watch his every movement as he pulls down his bathing suit to reveal his plump, rather large ass. Some blonde-ish hair is spread between his nipples, and those pink, supple lips – fuck.

He slowly turns to face me as I take off my bathing suit, too. We smell like salt and sweat and human and sex, somehow. All I want is to be in bed with this dude's skin against mine. Once he's naked I lay down on my back, and he just lays on my chest and stares into my eyes. I push him back a little and rub my fingers down his golden chest, around his nipples, then trace the contours of his defined abdominal muscles. Some people were simply born, but Nathan – Nathan was *designed*. He was carved out of stone for the specific purpose of driving my senses wild, of this I am sure.

We just lay there and stare at each other for a while, lost in wonder. I feel like there was a mountain range right outside my town that I never even noticed, never even bothered to explore. How could I have stared him in the face all these years and never noticed his muscular chest, his perfect jawline, the way his eyebrows frame his eyes like hawks?

"One more time," I say. "I know that going from friends to…more than friends is…murky territory."

"Murky?" he laughs. "Try awkward, and potentially explosive."

"True. Both true. But listen – I will be careful with your feelings, Nate. I promise. I will hold them like they're daisies, if you want."

He just smiles, then laughs again. "Yes. I do want that. But if you hold my *dick* like it's a daisy, I will be *severely* disappointed."

I laugh and get to work. "Now sit up."

No foreplay this time – I dive down and go straight for his balls, already my favorite part of him, even more than his dick. I just like the way they hang, I guess.

I look up as I swallow one ball into my mouth and wait for the look of heaven I already know will come over him, and it does. Fuck, I think I love that look even more than the hookup itself, when his mouth falls open and he closes his eyes and leans back, all thanks to me, and what I am doing to him...

Back to his balls. They are salty and a bit sweaty in a way that makes me fucking crazy. He also has this very human smell I would compare to something pheramonal – together the mix sends me over the edge. I reach up to his fat, seeping cock and start slowly pumping it as I suck his balls, licking and kissing and teasing. I feel him lean back and suddenly he's-

"Wait, are you already about to come?"

"Maybe," he moans. "It's just too hot – every time I get more turned on by it."

"Well, stop. I want to do something to you."

"What?" he asks me, red-faced.

"Penetration."

"What?"

"I wanna finger you, Nathan."

"Well, then – go easy on me. I'll try not to blow my load too quickly."

I keep lotion in my suitcase for jackoff emergencies in airports and such, so I reach over, hastily unzip it, and squirt some into my hand as I jack him with my other hand. Then I get him ready down there, looking into his eyes all the while.

"You sure?" I ask after a second.

"I'm sure," he breathes in a moan-y way. "I wanna feel my buddy inside me."

Holy. Shit.

I circle my finger around him. Take a deep breath. And go in.

"Fuck," he says, as my pointer finger rests about an inch inside him.

"What does it feel like?" I ask after a moment.

"Like...heaven?"

"Good. Get ready for more."

As I pump his cock, I move my finger in a small semi-circle, making him moan louder and louder.

"Oh, hell," he keeps saying. "Oh, hell."

I speed up a little, then start fucking him with more and more of my finger. He feels...different from a vagina, but not *that* different. The texture is just different, that's all. And tighter...

"Damn," I say. "You're way tighter than any girl I've been with."

"And your finger...it's...just, wow..."

"You haven't seen anything yet," I laugh.

"...But...how?"

"Have you heard of the prostate?" I ask him. "I Googled it once. They call it the G-spot, just like women have – we have it, too. And I can apparently reach it by doing this..."

Okay, so I've researched this once. I wasn't going to tell him, but sue me. It slipped out. I've been curious before, but I've never tried it on myself. Nate will be my first exploratory mission...

Very gently, I make a come-hither motion inside him, and his entire body clenches.

"Fuck!" he calls. He moves his hips faster and faster, and then he leans back and cries out.

"Stop!" he shouts. "Stop, or I'll come already."

"Whoa," I say as I remove my finger and he pants and tries to catch his breath, his legs clenched around me. "That was fast. But I want my dinner."

He stares down at me, his eyes exhausted and spent in a hooded, hungry way. "What's that?"

"Your come. Duh."

I can't wait anymore – I want to taste his cum. I want him in my mouth. So I lean forward and take him deeper,

deeper, deeper while tickling his balls at the same time, and then I insert a finger, too –

"Ahhh," he sighs. He squeezes me with his legs, opens his mouth, and spurts down my throat. I pump him for everything he's got, then finally swallow it all at once, savoring his taste on the way down. As he twitches and exhales, I lean up and kiss him, carried away by something I didn't even realize was coming.

"I want you to taste that cum," I say as we kiss. He's hesitant at first, then he gives into it again and kisses me back, and together we taste what he gave us. What I *made* him give us.

"How do you taste?" I ask, and he laughs a little and pulls his eyes away.

"Like…salt, and cooking oil. And sex, if that makes any sense."

"Whatever works," I say as I pull away and collapse onto the mattress for a nap. Fuck, I am never going to be able to contain myself around him again. I know I haven't seen many, but he's still got the prettiest cock I've ever seen. I already miss it whenever I'm not able to be with it. Even soft, hangs pretty low, and it's just wide enough to fit into my mouth (or so I guess). Perfect shape, perfect size…shit, even some glossy pre-come is dribbling out of the tip, already. Or is it post-cum?

"Junior prom," I let spill out of my mouth. He props himself up on an elbow and looks over at me, looking more beautiful than any dude has any right to look.

"Junior prom? What about it?"

"Well, once you were asking when I…if I've ever…if I've ever felt anything for a guy before. I did feel something for a guy. I felt it for *you*."

He smirks a little, but he still looks skeptical. "Explain?"

"Um. I remember we were posing for pictures in Kelly Mallett's backyard on the marsh, and I looked over at your hair and thought about how it was shinier than the sun, and I just…I just…"

90

There is a smile in his eyes that is not showing on his lips, so pink and wet. "You just *what*?"

I take a quick breath and turn away a little. "I wanted to curse your slutty little date out of jealousy, that's what I wanted to do. Now let's watch some TV together."

"Why?"

"Because I can't wait to wake up next to you in the morning, so I'm trying to get us to sleep early, that's why."

"Okay, okay. Just let me grab my diary first…"

what kind of love
from the diary of Nathan Sykes

I know I love him now.
I love him because
anyone would love him

(he is that magical)

I love him because
he just attracts love
like Venus
attracts the fly –

his laughter
makes my soul tremor
and his heart
is softer
than a baby's rolls

but where does that love live?

does it live
in the land of friendship
of video game sessions
and long lazy talks about sports teams
and friendly drinks at cozy bars?

or does it live
in the land of wild passion
and tender mornings
and gods and monsters and demons and angels?

basically,
what I want to know
for sure
is this:

how do I *love*
the one
I *love***?**

Nathan Sykes

That was the day the pact started to fall apart. The no-love agreement, I mean.

I know I said I wouldn't get attached. Obviously. I know I said it was only about sex. But things change. They change all the time. Oceans eat away at shorelines, reshaping the look of the coast. Seasons come and go, stripping trees and then making them bloom greenly again. And friends fall for other friends, finding new contours in each other they'd never noticed before. I know it's ludicrous of me to even be talking like this, about someone like Beau. But when I'm having the hottest hookups of my life with my best friend, it's natural for me to start getting a little...*fuzzy*, right?

Another evening passes, another series of hookups. Once he pauses the entire thing to demand that I stop touching everything else and exclusively lick his balls. At first touch he moans louder than he ever has before, and eventually he busts onto the side of my cheek. I absolutely love the feeling now – it feels so warm on me, so thick.

"What was that?" I ask as he blushes.

"Sorry, I…I just didn't know I'd like it that much."

"Don't worry about it," I say as I reach for a towel. "Actually, on second thought, I'm hungry…"

As he watches without breathing, I slide a bit of it into my mouth.

"Um, Nate?" he asks.

"Yeah?"

"That was the hottest thing I've ever seen, and I need to look away now before I catch on fire."

And that's only one hookup. It feels like our sex has simply become an extension of the rest of our dynamic, just an especially explosive one – like when an artist finally sits down to splash all of the colors in his mind out onto a white, clean canvas. Our canvas is just our bed sheets now…

There are other things. Once he gets a text from an old girlfriend that sends me over the edge, and I don't know exactly why. Then he checks out a hot, older lady in the hallway, and my mood doesn't recover for hours. This isn't right. We are just supposed to be each other's stand-ins for the girls who dumped us – we're not supposed to be the actual *girlfriends*. I have no right to be thinking like this, and I need to stop. It's not healthy. If I fall in love like an idiot, and we end up hating each other by the end of this trip, and I lose someone who is more of a brother to me than my own (much older) brother ever was...

I'll never forgive myself. I will honestly, truly never be the same person again.

That night Beau disappears to call his aunt, and I'm still a little buzzed from our group dinner. Soon I start feeling weird and possessive and controlling. Maybe it's the incident from earlier when his eyes trailed that lady's ass, maybe it's just the alcohol (which I replenish with the help of the mini bar). But my mind won't stop running, examining this from every angle...

I start wondering about his last girlfriend, the happy-go-lucky girl who seemed game for anything. Why did they break up? What happened? How did he fuck it up?

I pick up my phone and stare at her number. And I can't believe it, but soon I am calling Beau's ex-girlfriend.

"Hello?" Megan asks on the last ring, sounding confused but not impolite. I take a breath – I can't believe I just called her. Then again, I can. And I've got to speak now.

We were very friendly, after all, and in fact, on our group dates I'd usually chat with her more than Beau would. Ugh, just thinking about him right now sends a tingle down my leg...

"Hey," I finally say.

"Are you drunk?" she asks. I don't respond. "Seriously, what's up? Does Beau know you're calling?"

"Why would he need to?"

"Uh, I don't know..."

I still can't think of how to begin. Ugh. Awkward start.

"Anyway...yeah," I say, flubbing my words again. "Okay. Um. I was wondering, um...you know, I always liked you. What happened?"

"What happened? Is this Hillary Clinton?"

"No, I mean, sorry…between you and Beau, I mean. I was just thinking about it. What went wrong?"

"Oh. *That*." She exhales. "Random that you ask, but whatever. He just kind of…pulled away, I guess. Or, I mean, maybe he was never here at all…"

"In what way?"

"*Well.* You know how he is. He's a cipher. But with me, he was worse. I just felt like whoever he was, I never really knew him. I was good at faking it, but…I felt like a stranger to him. Why am I even admitting this? Ugh…"

"What were the good things, then?"

Her voice lifts. She gets that "aw shucks" tone to her voice that my own thoughts take on whenever I think about him. "The good things? There were a lot of them, I guess. He's smart and he works hard. He loves animals and kids so much. And he's *hot*…I was fending off bitches left and right. And he could be really good to me, really thoughtful. Actually, he was never *mean* at all. He was just…on vacation, in his head. But still, he could be so *warm*, too. Being around Beau Lindemann was like being around a bonfire. You couldn't help but get warm."

"Yeah," I say, my face burning with guilt and affection. She never un-loved him. It's so obvious. She just got too cold every time he stepped away. "I kinda know what you mean."

"It's actually funny that you're calling," she says soon. "It's funny you're asking all this. Well, not *funny*, I guess. I just always suspected this would happen."

"What?"

"This call. This conversation. I figured you were…*curious* about me. You'd study me whenever we'd all hang out, actually."

"Study you? Curious?"

"Yeah. You'd watch me."

I get a little defensive. "Why would I do that?"

"Don't ask me. But you two were like the same person. My friends always had this joke that I was in a three-way relationship, and I had to share Beau with you."

I know I should frown at this, but I smile. It melts my insides to think I had that sort of effect on him. It obviously makes me nervous, too.

"I don't know about that," I answer. "I guess we *are* good friends."

"Yeah," she laughs. "*Friends*. Whatever. Honestly, I thought you two always had some type of MSM thing going on."

"MSM?"

"You haven't heard of that whole thing? It's where, like, straight guys hook up with other straight guys. It stands for 'men who have sex with men.' Do you live in a cave?"

"Well, I'm pre-law, so…yes, I do."

"Whatever," she laughs. "Tell me, for real: why are you calling?"

"I, um…"

At this point I wish I could spill it out, I wish I could tell her that Beau paints the sky for me every morning and places the stars over the ocean in my head every night. But I can't. Nobody even knows about this. So I rush her off the phone and hang up.

But I can't get something out of my head – MSM. What is this?

I head to Google and soon get lost in some pretty interesting articles. It all has to do with the same subject I was researching before, I just didn't know there was a name for it. Apparently it's been a hot subject for sociologists and researchers over the past three or four years. First I find a study from a Scotland think tank that specializes in evolving attitudes regarding sexuality. It enlightens me on so much – for instance, there are all different kinds of MSM situations, and people come into this for all different reasons. One "straight" man in the study says his sexual appetite is so huge, he just hooks up with a guy if he can't get with a girl at that moment, and the researchers even gave him a lie detector test – and found he was being truthful. He really wasn't homosexual, at least not in his own mind. Another said he actually was attracted to men, but didn't attach it to any kind of sexual identity. A few identified as bisexual, a few said they were pansexual, but most seemed to shrug when asked for a label. A few even said they only care about the man's penis, and don't even look at the man it's attached to. (I guess this explains that weird "glory hole" thing, where a dude just sticks a penis through a hole and gets it sucked by a guy on the other side of the partition. If I had a dollar for every message I ever noticed scrawled on a bathroom stall saying "blowjob offered, no questions asked, just be here at midnight on Tuesday…")

But almost all of the guys in these interviews have one thing in common: they go through lives as what we imagine traditionally "hetero" guys to be. They drink beer and watch football with their hookup buddies. They drive pickups and wear camouflage hats. It seems that "gay" and "straight" don't even mean that much to them anymore.

The more I think about it, the more my head spins. Soon I find a New Yorker interview with an anonymous guy who hooks up with men on Craigslist, behind his wife's back:

Call it "bromance sex," call it a "bro-hookup," or even call it "dude-sex," but sociologists all agree on one thing: it's happening. From rural red-state cowboys to inner-city straight men with girlfriends, men who identify as "heterosexual" are having sex with other men in record numbers.

"As a man living in a society that suppresses gay men, don't you worry about what this makes you?" a journalist recently asked Marc, real name redacted, who enjoys casual hookups with certain male friends. "Is that why you decline to identify as a gay man?"

"No. Not at all. Why would it? That's exactly the point. We don't care about labels anymore. I like to suck dick, and that's it. Have you ever seen two girls get frisky and flirty with each other on the dance floor? It happens all the time. Sometimes they even make out. And what is the crowd's reaction? They cheer and yell and pump their fists. Meanwhile if two men enjoy each other, they're labeled as being sad and confused and closeted and in denial. What if we looked at women the same way we looked at men? How many more men

98

would admit they've felt things, too, instead of doing everything they can do hide it and deny their same-sex urges? How many men have even killed themselves because of our damaging views on all this, and the way we try to force everyone into these little boxes? My over-arching view on the subject is this: who gives a single fuck? This country would be a totally different place if it just stepped back and let people live their lives."

I sit back and decide he's exactly right. We're so hypocritical as a society. Women who experiment with other women are called fun and flirty and adventurous. Men who do the same with other men are called sad, desperate closet cases. Why did I never realize any of this before?

And I know, why don't these men just identify as gay or bisexual? But I think that's beside the point. One scientist says it's because men historically don't attach sex to emotion, like many women do. They're able to dis-attach the two, to basically fuck someone and then go on their merry ways – so they hook up with a guy and then keep dating women, like it never happened. Another researcher says it's because these men want the pleasure men can offer, but don't want any of the baggage of the "queer experience" – the persecution, the isolation. And I can't deny that this is a good point, too. I can't remember *one* popular kid from my high school who happened to be gay – they were all sequestered to drama classes or the arts programs. Many of the jocks wouldn't even talk to gay guys or associate with them. But then again, I know for a fact that those same jocks would get pretty damn flirty with each other in the locker room, slapping each other's bare asses and playing games of "gay chicken" where they'd touch each other and see who blinked first…the idea was that the first one to react to the touch was enjoying it, and therefore more gay than the other. But looking back, *what is more gay than literally hooking up with another dude to prove you're not gay*?!

And speaking of that – there's one more thing I need to know. I want to find out, definitively, how to reach my G spot, so I can play with Beau's, too. I want to do what he did to me. But I want to make it even better.

I find an article fairy quickly. "The Male G Spot," it reads. "Not just a myth."

I devour the text and find that the G spot refers to the prostate, like Beau said. When hit from the right angle, it can make you orgasm within seconds.

"I can't even let my man hit it from the back," one guy interviewed for the article says. "It makes me bust too quickly, and the sex is ruined right then and there. Nobody likes to be a two-second lay..."

There's a diagram at the bottom, instructing you on how to hit your own prostate. My pulse throbbing, I disappear into the bathroom, drop my shorts, and sit on the edge of the tub with my ass out. I squirt some lotion on my free hand, make sure it's good and soaked, and move closer to my hole...

I look at the diagram. Basically it tells you to move your thumb inside yourself, facing forward, and then to move it up and forward at the same time, toward your balls. I take a breath, make a face, and then...*bam*. I'm inside myself.

I moan a little. I'm still not used to this – it feels like I'm being stretched out, and my muscles down there still don't know how to handle it. It feels sublime, though – it's just odd.

My toes curling, I move my thumb in the motion described by the article – and then groan. Instantly it sends a warm, fluttery feeling throughout my whole body, and my core goes numb. It feels like my stomach is contracting and stretching at the same time, too – what is this?!

I do it again, and my eyes roll back into my head. I start hitting it harder and faster, then I put down my phone and start jacking my dick, too. Then I imagine it's actually Beau's big cock doing this to me, instead of my hand, and I imagine that he's bare, too. Just as I imagine him delivering a big wet load into my hole, I hold my breath, clench up, and squirt all over my right leg.

Damn, that was good...

When Beau returns twenty minutes later, I'm cleaned up and laid out on the bed like nothing ever happened at all. He smiles at me, and I smile back and take out my diary for my nightly entry. But his smile makes the most important question of the whole night sink into my soul. And at the end of the day, does all this "MSM" stuff mean I can keep fucking Beau without having to actually date him?

But at the same time: what if I actually *want* to date him?

hey Beau
from the diary of Nathan Sykes

Hey Beau Lindemann – I want you.

Hey Beau Lindemann – I'll never be strong enough to actually give you this letter, but I really do. I really want you. My eyes always find you in a room, and I catch your name flitting in and out of my mind from sunrise to bedtime. You haunt me in every beautiful way.

Hey Beau Lindemann, I know we're best friends, and I know we're standing two kids away from each other in the photo from Miss Underwood's kindergarten class. And I know we live in a place that looks at two boys holding hands and raises an eyebrow at best and raises a fist at worst. But I want you.

Hey Beau Lindemann – I know this was never supposed to happen. But if you didn't want me to fall for you, you never should've been born with dimples that deep, with a laugh that bubbly, with eyes that depthless.

And hey Beau Lindemann – I want you. I want you and I don't know what to do about it anymore…

Because I was born with the desperate need to send out a whole lot of love, but I've never found a worthy recipient. Until now. Until you.

So, hey Beau Lindemann – I want you to love me. Please say yes. Please say you do…

Beau Lindemann

I hit the streets early the morning after the group dinner, desperate for my muscles to feel the burn of a good cardio session. I head down the main tourist street then turn on a wide waterfront road, and soon Eminem is shouting into my ears and my legs are pumping and I'm in my zone.

I had to get away from Nate for a minute – I just had to. Things are happening so quickly, and I need to wrap my head around it all. Working out was always the jock-iest thing about me – if I don't exhaust myself at least once a day, I can't sleep. And if I don't sleep, my whole mood is wrecked the next day. An hour of cardio will do me just fine, though.

But the other reason I needed some time alone is...complicated.

Last night I dreamed I was marrying Nate.

Our families were there. It was like the "dream version" of the local beach, where it looks like the real version, but not *quite*. And we were getting married at sunset. Nate told me he didn't ever want to be with anyone else, and I said the same. I tried to look around and see if my mom was there, because she often shows up in the periphery of my dreams, but she seemed to be nowhere. And just before we exchanged rings, I was jolted awake and found it was just after dawn again.

I looked over at him then, and I can just remember this relief hitting me – *he's still here. He's right here.* And then I felt something else, too – guilt. Yesterday he made a comment I didn't like – he said he's starting to feel used. I know our agreement was literally built around us using each other, but I knew exactly what he meant. I once dated this man-eater of a girl, Jess, who made no secret of the fact that all she wanted from me was sex. She'd text me late at night, come over, fuck me, and then leave again. I always felt so...empty afterward. The idea of it sounded so cool from afar – *oh, awesome, a girl who literally only wants dick from me!* But the reality of it was so lonely.

So when Nate said it, I felt so bad for him, both as a friend and as...whatever this thing is becoming. At the end of it

103

all, he's still someone I care about, and it made me realize how automated I'm becoming – sex, sex, sex, with nothing else on the side. Our little moment in the sea was amazing, but it was just a *moment*. I don't want him to feel how Jess made me feel, like a sex toy that became human...

Speaking of sex toys, I spot a sign up ahead that stops me right where I am. I've run all the way to the seedier part of town, where Key West starts becoming whatever is west of Key West, and tucked into an old shopping center is a store with a huge sign in its blacked-out windows.

Adult Superstore, the sign says. *For all your steamiest adult needs.*

Hiding a blush, I cool off for a minute and then step inside. Due to that time when I went on a run and twisted my ankle and found myself stranded alongside a highway, I keep a debit card in my shoe when I run, and I take it out as I wander to the area obviously reserved for gay men. There are jock straps, whips, and leather S&M outfits with nipple clamps attached. I feel the heat on my cheeks as I slide on to the dildo section. My eyes zero in on one in particular – it's almost my exact size and shape.

My dick gets a little hard as I look at it. We're almost out of lube, anyway, so I need to make a purchase – why not try this out with Nathan? We've only got a few days left. Why not have some fun?

And I know it might not make sense, but why not use a sex toy to let him know that *he's* not only a sex toy to me? Attention is what he wants, and what I wanted from Jess, too. Why not give him some – in a way he would never, ever expect?

104

Nathan Sykes

I've just finished my morning "black coffee and scalding shower" routine when the door opens. I swivel around, naked, and sigh when I see it's just Beau.

"Geez," I begin, "I thought the maids were about to see my dick and my-"

"Shh," he says, walking forward, and the look in his eyes makes me stop short. "I got us something."

"But-"

"Hold on. Come here."

He peels off his shirt and pulls me against him. My body tingles as his scent hits my nose – it's sweaty and animalistic, and I have to fight back a moan.

"You know how exercise makes me horny?" he asks darkly. "Well, I passed a little sex shop, and, um..."

He reaches into a plastic bag and pulls out what looks like a replica of his own dick.

"Damn," I inhale. "Nice."

"Yeah. Come with me."

He pushes the extra bed, the one we stopped using when we started sleeping together, back into the corner, so it's against two walls. Then he jumps on it and sits in the corner facing me with his legs out. "What you waiting for? Come here."

"What's gotten into you?" I laugh as I crawl into bed. He grabs me, turns me around, and leans me against his stomach so we're both facing the same direction – and *facing the mirror, too*, I notice.

"I told you, cardio makes me crazy horny," he says against my shoulder, softly but dangerously. The tickling of his stubble against my earlobe makes me shiver as he opens up the package and lubes up the dildo. There's a heat building in my core, my face is burning, my throat is tight...what is he about to do?!

"So I was thinking, what would it feel like to do stuff to you while we both watch?" he whispers against my shoulder as he wraps our legs together. "I figured we could maybe get a little...sensual. A little romantic. In front of the mirror."

"But...I thought we were only hooking up as friends?"

His eyes lock into mine in our reflection. "That was before I knew what hooking up with you was like."

My insides jump. "*Oh.*"

"Yeah. So I figured we could do...*this.*"

I moan as he lifts up my leg and squirts some lube on me down there. Then he starts circling a finger around my hole as my muscles tighten.

"You like that?" he whispers as our eyes meet in our reflection again, five feet away. I can't even look – he's too sexy, and I'm too embarrassed of seeing my whole body close-up like this.

But at the same time, I can't look away.

He slips a finger into me, and with the lube it feels warm and wet and perfect. With his other hand he rubs my nipple as he works me.

"Fuck..." he keeps muttering under his breath. "Can't believe we never did this before..."

"I know..."

"But at the same time, I don't want you to feel used, or feel bad about this," he murmurs, rubbing my shoulder with one of his big hands as he holds the dildo with the other. "So I just thought you could use some...attention. Are you sore anywhere? Well, besides this little hole I keep abusing?"

"Um, my traps, from that workout," I whisper, red-faced, and he starts kneading against my traps as I close my eyes and moan. Fuck, this feels so good...

"No – open your eyes," he says, and I do as I am told – and our eyes lock in the mirror immediately. "Have you ever played with a toy?"

"Just with a girl – she wanted me to fuck her with her vibrator."

"Well now you're about to get the other side of things," he says, still massaging me. "Just watch."

Both of our bodies are in clear view – mine in front of his, and both of us are sweaty and tanned and toned from our workouts. It's quite a sight, I can't lie. As I moan again, he moves the dildo closer and starts rubbing the tip against my hole.

"Fuck…"

"Does it feel good?"

"Yes. Please fuck with me with it."

"What was that, now?"

"Fuck me with it! Please?"

"I may just have to do that," he says delicately as he rubs further down my shoulders. "Just after I rub these muscles some more." Who is this sensitive, romantic partner Beau has become? And why do I like it so much?

But I don't have any more time to think – just like that, he slips the tip of the dildo into me.

"Ahhhh," I exhale. I can see it enter me in the mirror, disappearing into me, and the sight alone makes me nearly convulse.

"Yeah, yeah – how's that feel?"

"Good," I breathe. "Different."

"Perfect. Now watch me fuck you with it in the mirror."

He leans forward and starts sucking on my ear as he rubs my neck with one hand and sinks the dildo deeper into me with the other. I don't want to orgasm, so I clench my jaw as I watch. The toy feels colder and harder than his dick inside me, but it's not bad at all – if anything it feels like it's opening me up, which I obviously need. He inches in, in, in, until the fake ball sac is against my skin.

"Fuck," he says softly, his eyes radiating desire, as he watches in the mirror. "I'm balls deep in you, aren't I?"

"Mhmm," I say, beyond words now.

"Now get ready to get fucked."

Without warning he thrusts it out a little, then back in. I cry out so loud, the vacuum cleaner in the next room turns off, and I hear some chatter in Russian.

"Looks like the housekeepers can hear," he smiles. "*Good.*"

He reaches around me and clutches me as he starts fucking me with the dildo harder. I moan and cry out again, even louder, as I feel it slide in and out of me. My mouth no longer belongs to me, and I don't even know what I'm doing – I'm screaming like someone is hurting me. But it doesn't hurt. It feels like heaven. And his eyes on mine, in this fucking mirror...

Harder, harder, harder. More, more, more.

Soon my legs are bending and my toes are curling and I'm feeling the heat and suddenly-

I cry out once, rock my hips back, and then bust all over my abs. One, two, three squirts, and soon I'm almost covered in my own semen. He groans, grips his dick with his free hand, and pumps a few times until I feel him coming all over the small of my back, and then it drops warmly down to my ass.

And just like that, it's all over.

"I don't even know *what* the hell that was," I laugh a minute later, "but I expect it again."

He looks at me in the mirror and gives me the cockiest smirk I've ever seen on him. It fits him, I must admit. "You got it, Pa."

"Pa?" I ask, and he just laughs.

"Just roll with it. I guess I'm breaking *all* the rules now."

~

"Hey, do you remember the fight in my fort?"

As we stumble back to the hotel room that evening, I laugh at his question. When we were about ten, we were playing in his tree house (known as The Fort) when we got into a tussle over who would play the captain of the war in our little game, and who would be the soldier. He pushed me down and I bit him in the arm, and we didn't speak for a week.

"Of course," I say. "I think my butt still hurts from being pushed down onto that wooden floor."

"Ha. I'm going to ignore the obvious joke I could've made with the butt thing."

I laugh again.

Quite simply, we had the perfect day today – after that explosive hookup with the dildo, we did our obligatory hangout session with the wedding crowd, and as soon as we could, we disappeared. We worked out together on the beach, doing free weights and sprinting drills, and now we're returning to the room after a stop at the fancy hotel bar. A woman hit on him, and he shrugged her off immediately and just smiled at me. It made me feel rather good, if I can say so myself.

"Oh," Beau says, "and do you also remember when we went to that Christmas parade in middle school, and that drunk lady threw little bottles of liquor at us from the float, and we got drunk together for the first time in my garage?"

"Ugh. I can still feel the nausea."

We take a shower together, but we're not being sexual – just kind of cute and affectionate, like how we were earlier. I like it even better than sex, to be honest, and I hope I keep seeing this side of him. When we're lounging in towels twenty minutes after the shower, I scroll my Twitter feed and look over at Beau.

"Hey," I say.

"Yeah?"

"So I was thinking…we should explore this thing a little more. We obviously both like guys, and we're in one of the gayest towns in the country."

"It is?"

"You mean you didn't notice all the rainbow flags and gay couples? Key West is *super* gay-friendly."

He shrugs. "Honestly, no. I never noticed this stuff before or looked for it – I guess that hasn't changed."

"Well, yeah, there are gays everywhere, actually."

He clams up. "Oh. I didn't know you were looking."

"Stop. You know it's not like that."

"What's the point of this, then?"

"I'm just…curious about all this. Let's look into it a little. Hey, what's the gayest thing you do right now?"

He blushes. "Sometimes I watch *Real Housewives.*"

"No!"

"Yep. What about you?"

"Well…I get two pedicures a month."

"Yep, that's pretty gay," he laughs.

"But I want to learn more. I've been reading up online, and it's only making me more curious. That's why I almost want to…"

"What?"

"Okay, fine, we're in the gayest town in Florida, and I wanna go to the gay bar. Are you down? I noticed one, like, two blocks away from here."

He raises an eyebrow. "*Really*?"

"A lot of straight people go, too, actually."

He shrugs. "True. And I mean…I guess it can't hurt anything. It's not like Lane and his goons will be at any of them." But then he gets more pensive. "But…what if we get hit on? How are we going to handle that side of everything? All we've done is hook up – we don't know how to be *gay*, in the social sense…"

"Chill," I say with a frown. "And I don't know. I'll be fine with you talking to someone, if you want to. And I won't be talking to anyone, so that's irrelevant…"

He bites his lip, and I can tell he's not at 100% yet, regardless of his words. "Well, then, I trust you. Lane and them are boring the hell out of me, anyway. Let's go to the gay bar!"

Some pre-gaming ensues, and at ten PM we are stumbling to a gay bar on Duval Street, Key West's main tourist drag. We pay a five-dollar cover charge in front of a big pink townhouse, then we walk through a beaded curtain into a dark, sparkly room. And then I discover an entire world I never even knew existed.

Until a few years ago, I thought gay dudes pranced around and spoke with lisps – I will fully admit that I was fucking *ignorant*. Now I know that those guys exist, and that's fine – but all types of other gay people exist, too. My main reference for gay life growing up was *Brokeback Mountain*, and not in a good way: I remember that for months after the movie came out, it was the joke everyone used with each other, *all* the time, when referring to gay issues. I only ever heard gay people being invoked to ridicule or mock or erase someone else – *that's so gay, you're such a fag, you're such a fairy,* etcetera. It made me think the only thing a gay person could ever be was a punch line. And if gay people weren't being made into jokes, they were simply being ignored – they weren't anywhere. They were hidden from public life like they didn't exist, when I'm learning more and more that they *clearly* do. Tens of millions of them, actually. Fifteen percent of the human population is said to be some shade of LGBT, according to that Scottish article I found, whether society wants to accept it and recognize it or not.

I never found myself exposed to any kind of gay environment, so I guess I was expecting something cheesy and clichéd. But this club...this is so different. As soon as we walk in we are blinded by a stage decked out in curtains made of white and pink tinsel. Three go-go boys dance on a platform between the bar and the seating area, and thumping disco music provides it all with a thrilling, sort of sexy atmosphere. But there isn't just *one* type of person – there are drag queens, but there are also straight girls, and men or every size and color, and people of unclear gender, too. You'd never find a variety like this anywhere else, actually, and *especially* not at a straight bar. I love it all immediately.

"Cool, huh?" I ask Beau, and I see he's just as enraptured as I am. We wait by the bar, since I don't think either of us knows what to do with ourselves. As we both watch, studying things, a hand appears on the bar, followed by a deep and attractive voice.

"Well hello there, stranger."

I look up and see a face I recognize instantly. Oh, shit – it's Genaro! Of course he would be here in Key West – he's good friends with the bride! I should've thought about the rest of the wedding group showing up, now that the weekend is almost here...

A friend from my freshman year of college, Genaro eventually "came out" as gay and quit my frat and never really came around again. Looking back, I can fully understand why he quit – those guys in the frat said terrible things, all the time.

111

I'd quit, too, just because of Lane alone. I don't think he's ever insulted someone before, for *any* reason, without including the word "faggot" in there somewhere as a nice little kicker.

Fuck. And I never realized how handsome Genaro was, either. He's tall, probably so tall it stops all chatter when he walks into a room because it's so noticeable. His nose has been broken a few times, but he has pillow lips and a huge black hairstyle like a 1950s teen idol. And he is suddenly looking at Beau like he has been lost in the Sahara and Beau is a pitcher of icy lemonade.

I reach over to break the spell. I don't hold it against him, though. I'm under that spell, too. It's only natural to become spellbound by Beau Lindemann.

"Um, Genaro. Hi. You were just talking to me, remember?"

"Oh, hey!" he says, remembering I exist again. "I thought I'd come over and say hi, since I'm in town," he says in his light Puerto Rican accent. "So...would you like to get a drink or something and catch up, or...?"

Suddenly I realize this is the perfect chance to do what I've been craving – get an insight into the world of being gay, and maybe even get some advice on how to make it work with Beau. (If we can make it work at all.) And we're still just friends right now, so why would Beau care if I left him alone for a minute? He *wouldn't* care. He can fend for himself for a while.

"Yes, but...let's go somewhere else," I tell Genaro. "Just for a minute, though. I need to talk, actually. Let's go now?"

"Cool, yeah. I was just on my way out. This place is lame."

I tell Beau to hold on, not even waiting to gauge his reaction, then head out the front door again with Genaro.

"So...what's going on?" he asks as we hit the sidewalk. "Why are you...um..."

"At a gay bar?"

He laughs and nods.

112

"Long story," I say. "Anyway, catch me up. What's been going on?"

Genaro goes on for a while about how he changed majors and had a breakup and various other things I can't really pay attention to. Soon enough, he notices how distracted I am.

Or should I say *dick*-stracted...

"So...anything you want to talk about?" he asks soon. "You're acting like you just saw a bald eagle roasting on a campfire."

"Oh, um, well the thing is...I need advice, and...well, it can only come from you."

"Tell me," he says.

"Well, first of all, I think I might want to date a guy."

I press my eyes closed for a moment, then open them – and he's just smiling at me. He doesn't look as shocked as I expected. This confuses me.

"...And?" he asks.

"What do you mean? Aren't you...shocked?"

He smiles harder.

"What?" I ask.

"I mean...should I be honest?"

"Sure."

"No, I'm honestly not that shocked."

"Okay. Why not?"

"Because you were a total womanizer when I knew you, and so was my Uncle Tom," he says more casually. "He is now married to his husband Eric with two golden retrievers, by the way. Sometimes it just works out that way. Also...you can wear the fuck out of a suit, too. And aren't you a big shopper? And a liberal, too?"

"Okay, fine," I sigh. "Maybe it's not *that* far-fetched. I don't think my family will react well, though. If I tell them, I mean. They have no idea."

"I understand..."

"I need help," I say, my words starting to tumble out of my mouth. "I have a plan to try it out, but..."

"Don't tell anyone about anything until you're sure," he says quickly, and with authority. "Let's start there. It'll change

113

your whole life, and if you're not actually gay or bisexual, it could lead to some complications."

"How do I know for sure what I am, then?"

"I actually knew a guy who was curious," he begins as we cross a street. "He came out as bi, then tried to date some guys – and he found he hated it. He didn't even want to hook up with them. So before you make an announcement or anything, you need to…investigate. I cannot underscore how terrible the Deep South is to any man who is not straight. Like, we're from *South fucking Carolina*, you know? So you need to be sure. You might be fluid, you might be straight, hell, you might be a huge flamer. But you don't know yet."

"Flamer?" I ask, confused.

"I'm a proud homo, I can use these terms. Anyway, the words mean nothing in the first place, to get technical. The term 'straight' isn't even really a real thing to me, technically speaking – I think everyone feels, or has felt, certain things in the past, but our vicious little society forces them to hide it and push it down. Because of that, we have this weirdly rigid view of gender and sexuality, when really all that is much less black-and-white than anyone will admit. You'd be shocked by the guys I've seen on these hookup apps on late nights when they've had some drinks and want to get away from their girlfriends for some experimentation…"

"Girlfriends?" I ask. He shakes his head.

"Like I said, don't ask. It's all so complicated. That's why I wasn't surprised when you told me. I've grown to just not think so much about it, and take things as they come." He takes a breath. "So who's the guy? Can I guess?"

I pause, then like lava from a burning mountain, I let it slip out in a hot desperate sentence: "Okay, yes, it's obviously Beau. I'm seeing Beau. He was…sort of burnt-out on chicks. So was I."

"I'll say."

"Hey. Don't laugh at me. I'm scared. The guys on the trip are being weird about it, and I don't know what to do…"

"Don't worry about those assholes," he says. "And honestly, I always knew."

"You did?"

"When I was in the frat, you two were always, like, weirdly...*territorial* with each other. That's the word. If I hung out with one of you, the other one would always come sniffing around, asking a little too many questions, being a little too curious. I mean, frat boys are always a *little* homoerotic with each other – what kind of straight guys touch each other's butts all the time, anyway? – but you two took the cake. And it was a very gay cake, with glitter and sparkler candles, too."

"Really?" I ask, dumbfounded that it was always so apparent to other people when it wasn't even apparent to *me*.

"Yep. You're lost, I'm afraid. I saw it in your eyes the second you told me his name."

"Ugh. Fine. I'll admit I am. But he's still my best friend, and obviously if this doesn't work out, it will completely change my life..."

"And if it *does* work out, it will completely change your life, too, in a different way. A *good* way."

"I know," I sigh. "That's why I'm scared, G. And I'm not an idiot – I know the world still isn't very kind to gay people, like you said. You guys couldn't even get married until a few years ago, for God's sake..."

"Tell me about it," he says. "Actually, no, don't even get me started."

I sigh. "Ugh. Okay, well, thank you for talking. I'll just...go with the flow, I guess, and hope it ends up well."

"Just keep it going – very quietly – until you get back to Charleston," he says encouragingly. "Then regroup and reconsider. That's my advice. That'll be the big decider – if you can keep it going after you take that big leap."

"Gotcha," I say, suddenly chilly.

"But remember to be careful, too, in the meantime. Not sure if you know this, but, um...your friends are, well, they're..."

"A bunch of bigots? Yeah, I get that. Thanks for reminding me, though," I laugh.

"Ha. Godspeed, good friend. At the very least, I hope this still gets you some amazing sex."

"Oh, don't worry, it already did. And geez," I add, "I forgot how funny you were. Why did I ever stop talking to you, again?"

We share a moment of awkward eye contact. *Shit.* Of course I know why we stopped talking – my entire frat turned its back on him, and I went along with it without saying a word.

"Look," I say soon, "I'm sorry about all that. Those guys were-"

"It's fine. It was preferable, actually."

"What do you mean?"

"Nathan," he laughs, "do you think that after I came out, I wanted to sit around for one second and listen to people like Lane say horrible shit about me all day? Please. And he didn't just talk about gays, either. He made fun of women, and black people, and Hispanic people, and…"

I shudder. "I know. You have a point. I'm already at the end of my rope with it, myself."

He appraises me, then smiles. "Well this is an interesting time for someone. Good luck, and have fun. And don't underestimate what a big life change this can be."

"I know…"

He looks away. "Um…I don't think you do, though. I wouldn't change anything about myself, but Nate…I can't hold hands with the person I like in public. People would stare, and it would just be uncomfortable and awkward. So we don't hold hands. Can you imagine what that's like, though, to *not be able to walk down the sidewalk and touch the person you love?*"

For a moment I try to compare this to what I've already dealt with. The way Lane and them are already looking at us strangely and skeptically, trying to figure out what's going on. In fact, they're looking at us like we're garbage.

But then I stop trying to understand at all. I can't comprehend what Genaro's life has been like at all, and it would be insulting for me to think I could. I've never dealt with it…*yet.*

"I'm sorry," I say soon. "I really mean that. I don't understand why people are the way they are. If I could change them, I would."

"I appreciate you saying that," he says warmly. "Like I said, I'm mostly fine with how I am. Oh, and by the way, go get your dude – *now*."

"Why do you say it like that?" I ask, and he just laughs again.

"Oh, young one – you have so much to learn. Beau Lindemann is hot as *shit*, and gay guys aren't going to let something like that stand alone in a bar for too long before they pounce."

And with that, I turn on my heel. *Nobody* else is going to talk to him tonight, that's for sure…

"Thanks, G! See you at the wedding!"

Beau Lindemann

I stand at the bar gritting my teeth and clutching my beer so tightly, I'm afraid it's going to shatter any minute. Where the fuck is Nate, anyway?

Look. I'm not jealous. I swear to God. This is just a hookup thing, anyway, and he just went on a walk with the kid, for Gods' sake. It doesn't matter. I'm just using him for sex while we're both here for a single-and-ready-to-mingle week in Florida, and that's all it is. If he wants to go hook up with other guys, that's on him. Whatever. I'm not envious at all. I'm just...

I'm just...

Okay, fine, I'm fucking jealous.

As I stand there ordering beer after beer, I become absolutely furious. I shouldn't be, of course, but I am. Because I want his hole to be mine. I want his dick to only be accessible to me. I want him to be...well, *mine*, like I said. I thought I had time to figure this out. I thought we had a few more days to explore all this, and for me to probably waffle back and forth and think about the fact that I know nothing in the world anymore because Nate is populating my dreams and my nightmares. But clearly we don't have any more time. That mile-high model dude from CofC is *clearly* in love with Nate. I don't think it's just me being paranoid – when they started talking, Genaro looked at Nate like he was on fire and Nate was an extinguisher. And then they left. What the fuck am I going to do now? Maybe this thing is already over, and tasting my dick gave Nate a taste for *other* dicks...

I spend half an hour in a blind rage, totally ignoring everyone around me. He shouldn't get to go run around with model dudes while I sit here, alone, trying to figure out what we are, and why this means so much to me. It makes me feel insane and possessive and very, very sexual, too.

When Nate finally returns, *alone*, I swallow a shot of whiskey and turn to him. I'm relieved Genaro is gone, but I still feel volcanic. "We're going," I say through gritted teeth.

"What?"

"We're going. Back to the room. Now."

"Um. Okay…? Why?"

"Because you're about to get your ass played with."

His eyes grow. "What?"

"I want to do things to you. More things than we already did. And now I'm going to. Because I'm mad. And you need punishment."

He grabs me by the hand and turns me around. "What are you doing, Beau? What is this?"

"He's definitely hot," I say as I smirk back at the doorway. "He aged well, that's for sure. Is he your new hookup buddy now?"

"He's…he's…"

"Oh, I get it – he's your boyfriend. That's why you're silent. I get it. I'll leave you alone now." I rip my hand from him and turn away, then turn back just as quickly. "How was it, anyway? Did you suck him off?"

"Stop, Beau. That's so crude. Don't talk to me like that."

"Well you liked him. Admit it."

He sets his mouth. "I *don't* like him. I won't admit to lies. Stop being crazy. All we talked about was how I've fallen for someone, and about how he always knew it, too."

My anger fades a little. "He did? And you…what?"

"He said we were always like this. And that he was pretty much just waiting for this to happen, basically."

I try not to smile. I'm a little flattered, but I still want to be pissed. "Well, fuck that. He doesn't know you. Maybe he's just obsessed. Maybe he's your stalker."

He rolls his eyes and blows out some air. "Beau, you're the one who was so intent on the pact including a clause about not falling in love. If we're just each other's sex toys, who the fuck cares about what I do? You can't have it both ways."

Shit. He has a point. There's no way I can claim to be mad if *I'm* the one who keeps reinforcing the fact that we're simply sexual partners. But losing control of my emotions like this tonight…I hate it, I absolutely hate it. And it makes me angry at *him* for having this power over me.

119

"Fine," I say. "I just…it was just weird, I guess. To stand here alone, to not know what you were doing…"

A smile creeps across his face. "Aw. Beau-Beau is jealous."

"I'm *not* jealous. This thing is just getting…weird." Suddenly I notice that he's staring down at my pants with large eyes. "Hey, what is it?"

"It's just…why is your dick hard right now?" he asks, horrified. "It's kinda distracting, when we're trying to fight…"

I look down and groan at my penis. Oh, God. When I get in this mood I am completely unable to stop myself. I always know what's coming, and yet I can never stop it. My temper is a boner trigger, and it's that simple. Tonight I am about to do one of two things: make a fool of myself, or hook up with Nathan.

"You're right. Sorry. Being mad makes me kinda…horny."

"Is that right?" he asks, laughing at me. But then I notice *his* dick, too, bulging against his leg, semi-hard. And that's when I realize what I need to do. I need to punish him in a different way. One that both satisfies my temper *and* satisfies my boner, too.

"I need to go to sleep," I say as I turn away from the bar and head for the door. "And don't worry – I already covered our tabs. So come with me – *now*."

Ten minutes later we're back in the room. This is getting more complicated by the day, by the second. We're either at each other's throats or on each other's lips. It needs to either stop, or become perfect. There will be no in-between with this.

But I can't stop now, and on the walk back here I only got angrier. The truth of the matter is that he still left me alone – he abandoned me in a gay bar, when we'd showed up together. Even if we were just friends, that would still have been uncouth. Where was he raised, anyway? A swamp?

"Don't touch me," I say when he walks up behind me. "I'm still your best friend. And I'm still bigger than you.

Remember when we got drunk last Thanksgiving and got into a fight in the backyard and I kicked your ass?"

"How could I forget? You chipped my front tooth."

"You chipped your *own* tooth."

I turn around, right at the end of the bed. His eyes roll up to the ceiling. "Yes, because that is my main hobby, causing expensive dental damage to myself. I love it. I live for it."

"Shut up. Don't tempt me. I'll do it again."

He doubles back. "Oh, so am I just some little bitch now for you to boss around, just because we hooked up a few times?"

"We won't do it again, I can tell you that much. Don't worry."

He leans in and puts a hand on my shoulder. I scoff, then slap it off. "*Don't* fucking touch me."

Anger shades its way into his eyes. He reaches out and touches my shoulder again.

"*Don't* touch me," I repeat. "I'll still fight you again."

"Fuck you."

"I already tried. You didn't want to. Remember? After the pool the other day? You said you were too tight."

This time, he *slaps* me in the shoulder. My eyes narrow. I reach over and push him, too.

"Fuck you, bro. You're annoying."

He growls, and before I can even register what is happening, he's rushing forward and pushing me backwards. Emotions have been simmering under the surface for days, complicated ones, and I can feel them exploding every second. We both fall onto the bed, and I fight back by wrapping my arms around his shoulders and trying to immobilize him. But he's too agile, too slippery, and he shimmies away and elbows me in the ribs.

"Fuck you, asshole!" I cry as we begin writhing and wrestling.

"No, fuck *you!*"

My shirt comes off in the madness, and I ignore the tingles I get from my skin being against his clothing as we fight. I push him up against the headboard and slap him in the

121

face, and he lunges forward, tackles me, and gets me into a chokehold. We're fighting now, full-on wrestling like brothers, and I kick and punch and elbow, just trying to keep him away from me. He's so mad, so angry, so *passionate*...

"What's your fucking problem?" I ask as he kicks me into the bedside lamp, knocking it over. I retaliate by wrapping my legs around his neck.

"You like me," he says soon. "You like me and you can't handle it and so you're angry."

"Fuck you."

"You know I'm right," he says. "Fucker."

"Prove it."

We stop, mid-wrestle. "How would I do that?" he asks. I pause and stare into his eyes. My libido has run away from me. I'm pulsing with an energy I've never known before, but somehow I trust it. This anger has triggered a sheer sense of kinkiness I didn't even know resided in me...

"The condoms we got at the gas station are on the bedside table," I growl. "Let's duke it out. If you win this fight, you can fuck my ass. If I win, I fuck yours. If you really like me, fight me so hard, you win my ass."

He glances over, sets his mouth, then looks back at me. "Fuck you, this isn't a game," he says as he slides away, but then he fakes me out and charges me again and pins me against the headboard. I try to move, I try to do anything at all, but I'm trapped.

Shit, that was good. Seems like I was too drunk to finish the fight I caused, and I just lost. I try to push back again, but I can't – he's in the perfect position against me. I should've remembered how strong he was when I challenged him...

"Fuck," I whisper. It's already over.

"So you really want this ass fucked?" he asks. "Looks like I won. Time to reap the spoils."

I hold his eyes with mine. "You won't do it," I say, testing him. I'm drunk and sloppy and I don't know what I'm doing, but I trust it at the same time – it just feels right to follow my emotions right now.

Keeping me pinned with one arm, he reaches over with the other and grabs the condoms and lube. I try to reach up, but he pushes me back.

"Nope. You lost, bitch. You're mine now."

I moan, overcome with passion.

"And I'm not taking off my clothes, either. You're about to feel my clothes against you as you get fucked."

I groan more quietly as he whips out his dick through his fly, slides on the condom, and yanks down my jeans a little. My legs are now around his shoulders, and we're in the perfect position for this to happen. But do I want it?

Our eyes meet again, and the jolt that shakes my body tells me the answer.

"You shouldn't have been so mean," he says, positioning himself against my hole. "Now you're about to pay the price."

He pushes his hips forward, and I scream as his tip opens me up. I squirm backward, and concern creases his face as he watches.

"*Ahhhh*," I moan. "I'm fine, that was just...tight."

"I know it is. But it's the price you've gotta pay, right?"

"Just shut up and fuck me. Please, Nathan. I earned it."

"Call me Mr. Sykes."

"Okay, Mr. Sykes, sir. Please fuck this ass."

He pushes forward again. It burns, but it also feels better than anything I can remember feeling in my life – I feel so full, so satiated, so satisfied. And the fact that it's my *best friend* inside me, the person who knows me better than anyone...fuck...this is just *so* intimate. I can't even imagine feeling closer to anyone, for any reason.

He pulls me up by the waist, arching my back for me. How does he know how to do this so well? Did Genaro teach him? That fucker...

Before I can think any more, he leans into me again – and I make a sound I never knew I could make, something between a scream and a sigh.

"Yes, fuck me, fuck me harder!"

123

"You got it," he says, and I look down at his Oxford shirt and his khakis against my sweaty skin. He's even still wearing his shoes as he fucks me, slowly at first, and as I start to lean into his thrusts, he goes harder and harder…

"Oh fuck, Mr. Sykes…oh fuck, Nathan…yes, my man…"

His name becomes a chant, a hymn, and he is my captor, giving me the punishment I asked for. I enjoy the dynamic so much, actually, a thought comes to me.

"Slap me in the face while you fuck me," I grunt soon, and I have no idea where it comes from – it just rises out of nowhere. I feel so aggressive, I just want to be fought again.

"Fine, bitch," he says, slapping me lightly in the cheek as his big dick fucks me. "How do you feel for trying to fight me? Do you feel bad? You should."

"Yes, I do," I moan subserviently.

"Say it louder," he demands, slapping me harder. "Now, bitch."

"I'm sorry for fighting my man," I whisper, and then I open my eyes – I can't believe I just called him that. But he doesn't seem to notice.

"Good," he says, slapping me once more, then grabbing my ass cheeks from the back and plunging in harder than ever. Fuck, it's too much – the passion, the anger, his balls slapping against my ass…

I lean back, cry out in a choked tone, and then bust all over my bare chest. He pulls out of me, then gets closer and squirts all over my chin. As I look up and watch, his chest heaves and his tendons twitch as he unloads all over me. It feels warm and sexual on my face, and I love every minute of it.

When he's finally done, he just smiles down at me, panting.

"What?"

"That ended differently from our Thanksgiving wrestling match, didn't it?" he asks, laughing, as he reaches over for a towel for me.

"You could say that. I don't remember getting dicked down after I drunkenly tackled you into some marshland and ruined your phone."

"Let's make sure they all end like this in the future, yeah?" he asks.

"How about no fights at all, actually?" I smile as I wipe off my face. "Just sex."

"I can get behind that," he smiles, his face happy and thoughtful again. "*Literally*."

Nathan Sykes

The next day's breakfast is a little awkward and tense – and *charged*. In the electric sense, I mean. He is either glaring at me or making eyes at me, and he doesn't even care anymore if anyone notices.

"Would you like any more of that sausage?" the server asks at one point, and Beau leans over and interjects before I can say anything.

"Oh, yes, he would *love* some – but make it sausage from another company," Beau says. "He *loves* to jump around, where his sources of sausage are concerned."

But his attitude only lasts so long. That afternoon we're all scheduled to explore downtown Key West before meeting up at the famous sunset spot, Mallory Square, for drinks and dancing and other tourist-y activities. At first Beau and I discuss going alone, and not really associating with the wedding crowd, since people have been whispering about how we've been a little absent lately. But after we agree to stay far away from each other for the day, he gets this cloudy look on his face.

"What's wrong?"

"It's just…I have to be with you," he says. "I don't feel like me without you."

I just stand there for a moment, dazed. But at the same time I completely understand. It is becoming a nuisance to be around anyone but him. My world is shrinking, and he is becoming the star of my mini-universe.

I smile as casually as I can. "Well, then. It's settled. Let's go together!"

Downtown Key West is just as I expected it, pretty much: rows and rows of Victorian mansions with an insane amount of bars and palm trees and tropical flowers in between. The public beach at the end of the highway is gorgeous, too. We start out down the main drag, which is full of grimy bars and grimier tourist shops with tacky shirts on display that say things like MOM'S OUT TO PLAY! and SOUTHERN GURL 4 LIFE.

But on these streets, something keeps happening. When I look over at him, I don't really see Beau, the guy I'd play video games with until three in the morning, laughing and drinking beer and talking about the previous weekend's hookups. I don't see Beau, the guy I'd get into fistfights with three or four times a year when we were young and dumb and full of testosterone. I see Beau, keeper of the light, the newest, shiniest thing in my life, the person I suddenly want to get to know on the deepest level imaginable, not so much the apple of my eye as the apple *orchard* in my eye.

He is not just one piece of fruit anymore, he is the whole tree...

I tell Beau I want to visit the house of Ernest Hemingway, my writing hero, and he shrugs and agrees. But whatever I was expecting Hemingway's house to be, it isn't what we find. Instead of some dark, masculine writing shack, it's a light, airy mansion full of lace and plasterwork and chandeliers. What surprises me most is his life story – he was a drunk and a womanizer, and none of his four marriages seemed particularly happy. How could you try *four* times and still not make your match?

"His portraits are so sad," I say in what looks like his study. "He looks so...lost."

"What do you mean?" Beau asks.

"It's just so sad – all his life, with all this success, he never found happiness. He never found real love. He even slept with the light on, because he was scared of the dark." I swallow. "I've read a lot of articles that said he was actually secretly gay, and that was why he tried to be so hyper-masculine, and never found happiness with any of his four wives."

"I don't know about that..."

I turn to a portrait of a sad-eyed young Hemingway and shake my head. "Hmmm. I'm not so sure..."

After touring the pool and gardens and listening in on a tour guide's stories about Hemingway's hilariously melodramatic love life, we finally meet everyone at Mallory

127

Square. The scene is…it's breathtaking, really. The Square is a huge area on the water filled with dancers and performers and tents selling tacos and margaritas and all kinds of weird little things, and it all faces the most beautiful sunset I've seen in years. All sunsets look the same, and nobody needs to describe them – until now. Until this one. This is somehow different. It looks like a melting pile of rainbow-hued sherbet, splashed out in the sky for all to see.

The wedding group is already being drunk and belligerent, though. I can barely deal with this whole crew anymore even when I'm *sober*, and when I see stupid Lane in his suspenders and red baseball hat, I feel like hiding. But we can't be too rude, so we spend ten or fifteen minutes enduring him shouting at passing women and hollering for no reason at all. Can this dude even survive without taking up all the space in an area, or what? Is anyone else ever allowed to get a word in?

Finally, I feel the familiar pull of Beau drawing me in, and we veer off the main square and follow some sounds to a ridiculously cool flamenco-type restaurant in a brick courtyard. People are dancing like they actually know how to dance, and the air smells like flowers and vines and tequila. A waiter sits us in a corner, which is secluded but also unfortunately next to a leaky faucet. But the small plates we order make up for the dampness – the food is amazing, every bit of it. I feel something starting to shift between Beau and me – our dynamic is changing. We're not really hanging out as friends anymore. It feels closer, more personal, but also a little awkward at the same time. Actually, if anything I am behaving like I'm on a date…because what first date *isn't* awkward?

And then I gasp and realize what this is – I am on my first date with my best friend in the world.

We eat in comfortable silence for a few minutes.

"Hey. You know we're closer to Havana than we are to Miami right now?" I ask soon. "That's why there's such a strong Cuban culture here. I've been reading all the tourist guides."

"Ugh," he says quietly as he drinks his burgundy wine. "You're so smart. I hate it."

"So are you, Mister Dean's List."

"After the last year of whoring and partying?" he laughs, and a light dances in his eyes that is downright offensive in its cuteness. "No, sir. Not anymore."

"Call me sir again," I say quietly.

"Why?"

"Because it was fucking hot."

His eyes change. The wine slides around in my stomach, and mixed with the lights and the music and the way his leg muscles look in his khaki shorts, I'm feeling a little bold. Who cares if someone sees us here? We're strangers in a sea of tourists...

So I put my hand on his leg.

"Wow," he says. "Really?"

"*Really*. Who cares?"

"I mean..."

"I know we're friends," I say, seeing his hesitation, "and I know it could go badly, but who cares right now? Anything could happen. Right?"

"God," he says, staring at my mouth for some reason.

"What?"

"I just really want to fuck your ass right now."

"*Whoa*," I say, sipping some wine again with bug-eyes. Looks like I'm not the only one who's feeling bold tonight.

"Seriously," he says, desire in his voice. "I want you so badly. Here, I'll guide you. *This* is what I want to do to you."

He puts a hand on mine (which is already on his leg), slides it upward, and before I know it, our hands are sliding up places where no hand should ever slide in public. Together.

Oh, I think. *Well, then. This is new.*

Then he leans into me, putting his lips almost against my ear. (Thank God we're in a dark corner and almost totally out of sight.) His stubble against my lobe combined with his low, breathy voice in my ear is enough to make my whole body go numb.

"Let me fuck you," he says. "Long, slow, romantic. Please? I need it so badly."

"What is this?" I ask, smiling. "Who are you becoming?"

"I don't know any more than you do."

I sit back, my head spinning at all this. "*Seriously...*"

"What?"

How do I say this? We only have a few days left here. What are we going to do when we have to go back to the real world, and...and this maybe falls apart? It could be awkward forever...

Finally he returns his back to his chair and frowns a little. Realizing I'm killing the mood with my self-doubt, I try to regroup. I screw up my face and decide to bring up the MSM thing.

"Hey. This is kind of common, did you know that?"

"What do you mean?"

"A lot of straight guys are hooking up with each other on the down low these days. I know it sounds weird, but there's been an epidemic of it lately – a lot of sociologists are even studying it."

He smiles, then looks away with a blush.

"What?" I ask.

"I never told you this, but remember that dude, Ryan?"

"The one who did crew? Yeah, why?"

"He asked me to do that. He used to hint about it a lot, actually."

"*What?*" I ask.

"We were suitemates freshman year. If we'd ever end up drunk in the common area late at night, he'd mention how he would get with guys sometimes, just to 'blow off steam' and 'relieve stress' and stuff. I never really thought much of it. He wasn't the first guy to hit on me, that's for sure..."

I glance away. "I don't want to know. I'll get jealous."

"Sorry. We never did anything. But anyway, the thing that struck me as strange was that Ryan was so...*straight*. He's even married to a girl now, but I'll still get a late-night text every once in a while where he'll ask me to meet up. And I really don't think he's *gay*, either – I think he just enjoyed penis sometimes. I mean, girls do stuff with each other all the time…"

"I know."

"What do *you* think about it?"

I sip some wine, then swallow. "I think…I think I would risk anything to feel how I've felt the last few days, Beau. That's all I know for sure. …What about you?"

He pauses, then clears his throat as the candle-light dances across his beautiful face. "I feel like…I feel like I was riding in a plane and I just got pushed out the door."

"So I'm killing you?" I laugh.

"No, Nate. You're making me fly."

For a moment I can say nothing. He has knocked me senseless.

He looks away, swigs some wine, and smirks.

"What is it?" I ask.

"When you talk to me this way, it just…turns me on. Even more than before. Not in a dirty way, but in a…*sensual* way."

"Me, too," I whisper. "Liking you makes me horny."

"Good," he murmurs. "Don't think that just because I'm not experienced at this, doesn't mean I can't still do things to you that will make you forget you're alive."

I freeze. "And what, *exactly*, would you want to do?" I ask quietly, almost fearfully. His eyebrow trembles a bit, but *just* a bit.

"Things that are not usually done in Hemingway novels, let's just say that." He lowers his voice and makes sure nobody can hear. "But…are you sure you're ready to switch off and take my dick? It's a big one…"

My insides jump, but I nod.

"Good. Now get the check, please. I can't wait any longer for you."

131

Beau Lindemann

We've barely made it into the room before I am smothering him in kisses. I don't want him to be able to even get any air right now, just to kiss me. *Just kiss my lips.* That's all. Oxygen is secondary when you're feeling as bright and as bubbly as this. I know it goes against our pact, but there can be no fighting a level of The Feels like this. Fuck the pact.

Obviously, though, I also want him physically, not just romantically. I just feel like our bond explodes to new heights whenever we're doing sexual things, deepening our emotional connection in the process. So with that in mind, I push him down on the bed face-first and command him to slide off his shorts.

"Yes, baby," I say as I watch him. "Yes..."

Damn, his hole is looking good as he bends over for me. The backs of his legs are covered in a light sheen of blonde hair, and the slightly sweaty smell from today is just making it all better...

I lean forward and kiss him right on his hole, spreading his cheeks as I do it. He responds with a full-body shiver. "Damn, I can't wait for this tight little hole to be mine."

"Fuck yeah, dude," he moans. "Play with it. Ugh, I love this."

I lick around for a few minutes, and soon he's leaning all the way into the bed, groaning as I explore him.

"You ready for my finger?" I ask. "I licked you to open it up. Shouldn't burn as much this time."

"How are you such an expert already?"

"...Um, I fucked Alyssa in the ass."

"The girl from last summer?"

"That's her."

"Ugh. I hated her," he says.

"Why?"

He looks back at me. "I don't know. I just did. And yeah, I'm ready, fuck me. Just be careful with me."

A smile stretches between us, twin grins twisting our lips. "Oh, you *know* I will."

133

I kiss his hole again, deeper this time. Every time we hook up it makes me bolder and braver. At first I couldn't even really admit I liked this – now I am getting more and more secure in my attraction to him. And the attraction is just growing stronger and more volatile...

I push out his legs and eat him out. He is pink and a bit hairy, but not much – and fuck, I love this even more than with women. I used to fucking *love* to eat a good, pink, tight pussy, but this is so much better. The sounds he makes, the way his face contorts with joy – *fuck*.

I slide on a condom, then lean into his ear as I lube him up. Most people think missionary is the most intimate position, but for some reason I want to fuck him from behind while laying on top of his back – this gives me access to his neck and shoulders and ears, my favorite parts of him. And not to mention this view of his perfect ass...

I lean in and whisper one last thing. "I don't want to fuck you, by the way. I want to have sex with you."

Then I grip him by the shoulders and push myself in.

"*Fuck!*" he cries.

"What?"

"Dick...too...big...must...slow...down...remember, I've never done this..."

Some impulse drives me to suddenly lean in and kiss his head. "Okay, sorry, babe. You got it."

He looks back. Our eyes meet as mine bulge out of my head. What was that?

"Oh, sorry," I say.

"Don't be sorry. Your dick is already in my ass. It's okay. Now *fuck* me."

Slowly I thrust once, then twice, taking a moment to soak in the fact that I am fucking my best friend. This plump ass, this tight back, it all belongs to Nathan Sykes, and the dick I'm seeing plunge into him right now? That's mine. We're really doing this...

"How do you like it?" I ask Nate, nipping his ear.

"Fuck, I'm getting used to it...here, let me finger you, it'll make you feel so much better..."

"Better than I do right now?" I grunt. "Impossible."

"Just wait," he says, reaching back and around. "I'm gonna play with your G spot. I just Googled how to reach it."

I feel a tightness, a pinching down there I've never experienced before, and then *bam* – I feel him in me, and it is a revelation. Then he does this strange movement, and the sensation is only heightened.

"Fuck. Ugh, yes, finger it. Finger my ass..."

Suddenly my mind fills with a series of images. European frescoes on cathedral roofs, full of angels and sunbeams and celestial clouds...choirs full of exalting children in gigantic churches...the most beautiful sunset in the world, multiplied by a billion...

That's how good his finger feels against my prostate. Tell me, again, why in the living hell we ever waited so long for this?!

My dick is in him, his finger is in me, and my tongue is in his left ear. I hold my breath and then accidentally bust then, images of heaven filling my mind, and then he does the same onto the sheets. This time, though, I lean over and slurp up just a bit of it. Then I kiss him.

"Don't think you were going to get away from that," I laugh into his mouth. "I'm officially going to taste you every time now. Just accept it."

"Trust me," he pants, "I don't think that'll be a problem..."

And soon we fall asleep around our wet spots, both of us sickened with the knowledge that in two days we will have to start making the biggest decisions of our lives...

free
from the diary of Nathan Sykes

you are
the best thing
I have ever found
in this imperfect world

you belong
in the most perfect of lands

you belong
somewhere you can fly
in free, clean air

but I know
you're scared
of what is happening
between us

and you deserve
the space to soar
without having to worry about
who's watching you fly

so darling
I know you're hesitating
and if your own heaven
isn't with me

I'll set you free
I'll watch you fly
and I will smile

because the only thing harder than seeing you leave
would be holding you here
and knowing
I am the thing

holding you down
and keeping you
so far from
your own heaven...

Nathan Sykes

The squaw of a seagull wakes me, gently but wonderfully. I open my eyes and see the curtains flowing in the breeze from the open glass door, and Beau is standing on the deck with his arms against the railing, holding some coffee. Beyond his tanned shoulders stretches the pastel sea, and above him, palms fan out into the sunlight. I roll over and feel myself smile. Sometimes I used to wake up already dreading the day; wondering what drudgery the world had in store for me. But today, I feel alive from my toes to my eyeballs. My limbs are nimble and free, and my eyes and brain are clear. I feel like I just woke up from a sleep that lasted years. Where have I been?

And how can I make this feeling last forever?

Of course, duty calls soon. We're supposed to get our tuxedos at this formalwear store across town, and while I don't want to have my solo time with Beau intruded upon by all these boorish, ignorant dudes, c'est la vie, right?

We all pile into a big van, and Lane passes around a flask containing an alcoholic liquid that is brown and warm and completely disgusting. I'm sitting directly next to Beau, which doesn't bother me at all – and when I study him I decide it doesn't seem like he cares, either. After all, we're still best friends – this shouldn't be any different from our usual behavior, right? Nobody will notice anything weird.

Except it doesn't stop there. Soon his hand falls on mine, which is on the seat with my fingers open. I just smile and breathe, comfortable with the knowledge that this is exactly where I need to be, and exactly who I need to be with. So what if I'm not sure if Beau is meeting me one-hundred-percent right now, mentally speaking – right now, this feels perfect.

Then something terrible happens: in the split-second before he takes his hand back, Lane spots us and turns bright red before glancing away.

I want to think this is nothing, but the damage is done. We've been spotted. Soon Lane's eyes lock with mine again, and I am positive that I see a smirk on his face. Oh, fuck. He was the last person I ever wanted to deal with. But at the same time, I know I can't just ignore him, either…

"So…" Lane says at the tuxedo place, when we're alone. My face goes red.

"Yeah? So, what?"

"You know what," he says, stone-faced. "What was that earlier?"

"I…don't know what you mean."

He smirks. "I thought I saw you…hmm, never mind."

I swallow. "No, you can say it."

"You were touching Beau. You were kind of…holding hands."

I keep my face impassive. I won't let him win this. "It's interesting that you think you saw that," I finally say.

"Yeah? So…what's the deal?"

I stare straight ahead. I know how to deal with guys like this – they want me to play along, to prove to them that I'm *just another one of the guys.*

"Are you guys…I mean, are you…a *thing?*" he asks, half-jokingly. I'm sure my face is the color of his big red plastic watch, but I just shake my head. I feel no shame about this, but at the same time I'm in no position yet to go around talking about it. Especially not when I don't even know what "it" is…

"We're not a *thing*. But…"

"Yeah?"

I swallow. "Even if we were, maybe we wouldn't say anything."

"What?"

Be strong, Nathan Sykes. Don't lie. There's no reason to lie here.

I turn to him and put on the "bro factor" and pretend it's all a big joke. "Dude. We're on vacation. Maybe things happen…maybe we're sick of Tinder girls ditching us for someone else every time their phones buzz with a better match. Yeah?"

"But…"

"But nothing," I smile. "People mess around all the time. It happens."

"Gotcha, then," he says, with the most patronizing wink I have ever seen. "Just be careful. We *are* from the South, after all…"

I try to ask him what he possibly means, but by the time I can form words, he's already gone.

My pulse picks up. I can't tell Beau because I don't know what to say, so I don't. But what does this mean? And what does he want from us?

All I know for sure is that right now, I've *got* to get out of here.

Hey, my friend Harrison says as soon as we get back to the hotel, **the bride and groom are greeting family all day, so we're off the hook. Some of the boys are going to Sloppy Joe's, that tourist bar – you and Beau are welcome to come.**

I read the text aloud, and one look between Beau and me tells me we're not coming. But after the incident earlier, I want to get as far away from here as I can. This place is toxic, and the walls are closing in. And part of me shudders to even imagine what would happen if Lane does something about this…

"What do you say about going for a ride?" I ask Beau.

"As long as you're there, I'm there, too."

We walk to a Hertz and rent a Chrysler convertible that is nearly twenty years old, and it shows every day of its age, too. We do manage to get the top down, though, and soon it is smooth sailing. Then we follow Google Maps out of town.

The Overseas Highway is a hundred-mile-long, mostly-elevated road that connects the islands of the Keys, and when it's not meandering through tiny little beach towns, it's a series of bridges through the most sparkling waters you've ever seen. Sometimes mangrove swamps jut out from the turquoise seas, and sometimes you're driving over sand flats so shallow you can't tell what is solid ground and what is ocean. All in all, it's a paradise in pastels, and speeding through with Beau beside me in an open-air convertible is almost too much, almost *too* perfect.

"You know what's weird?" I ask him at one point. I still can't get used to how blue-green the water is here. No matter how many times I stare at it, it's still beautiful. Beau and the Keys have that in common...

"What?"

"I thought you were one of my best friends, or my *very* best friend, but lately I'm realizing I barely knew you at all."

"In what way?"

"Well. I feel like I knew you on such a...*platonic* level. That's so different from what's happening now."

"Hmm. I guess I was...maybe hiding parts of myself?"

"So was I, probably."

I shiver. We're not touching each other, but his energy is still filling the air.

"Favorite food, besides mixing up side dishes?" I ask. "I feel like I've forgotten that."

"Cereal, but only with warm milk."

"Wow. Strange. And gross."

He shrugs. "You?"

"Steak and white corn. Never yellow corn."

"Oh, I already knew that. You always try to order that at Outback. And they never have it, either."

"Well let's find things you *don't* know, then."

We go back and forth for a while, and soon I feel more secure – we're really getting somewhere, somewhere beyond where we were before. When we're discussing the best and worst movies we've watched together at that trashy little theater in the shopping center in Charleston, I realize we have no idea where we're going. At a gas station we ask someone for the nearest tourist landmark, and he directs us to Bahia Honda State Park, an apparently pristine white-sand beach that overlooks an old bridge that fell apart. The guy takes out his phone and shows us a picture. One side of the bridge has become a platform where local teens jump thirty feet into the water, and just looking at the photo gives me the willies – but

141

Beau, of course, can't be contained, and forces me to drive him there.

The beach is just as advertised – actually, the water is even lighter than described. It makes the brownish oceans of South Carolina look like vegetable soup in comparison. We walk down the shore for a little, and all the while I'm trying not to notice Beau's muscular legs, his near-brown skin, the thin dark line of hair disappearing into his bathing suit and leading to his thick cock…

Ugh. This shit is *hard*.

Soon I hear myself laugh.

"What is it?"

"It's just…well, I literally wouldn't rather be with anyone but you right now. Not my family, not anyone. Is that weird?"

"No," he smiles. "You were *always* the one I wanted around for good times. And bad times, too, come to think of it. Remember when my dad died? Your house was the first place I drove. All I wanted was to sit on your loveseat and not think about a single thing."

"I remember. At the time I didn't get it, but…I mean, I guess I do now…"

"Yeah," he laughs. I take a breath.

"Speaking of that, did you ever pick up on any…signs?"

"What do you mean?"

"Signs that you were maybe…curious for me, or gay for me, or whatever this is?"

"Hmmm…no," he says suspiciously quickly.

"Come on – there have to have been points where you knew. Or even about *me*, and how I felt. Be honest."

He blushes. "I mean…you did get really into Britney Spears videos as a little kid, and not in a gawky, *she's hot!* way, but in a way where you'd sing along to the words and sway to the beat."

"God. I didn't know I did that. But at the same time, let's admit it – she did have some jams."

He throws his hands in the air. "Hey, not knocking Britney here – *Toxic* was the official song of one entire summer. She's a legend."

"Shit," I laugh. "Maybe we actually *are* gay. Can't get much gayer than Britney Spears fans, right?"

"Shut up," he says, then gulps. "Did you ever notice anything about...*me*?"

"Of course."

"Like what?"

"Well. There were little looks, little vibes I'd get...remember Fletcher McMahon, our old buddy from school? You'd stare at his ass all the time."

He starts to object, but I wave him off.

"Hey, not hating on you at all – that kid did have a *good* fucking ass. I mean, the sight of him in those baseball pants would make every single mouth drop on the stands. It was just unfair, really."

"True. Women love asses."

"So do we now, apparently, too," I laugh. "Oh, and...no offense, but your closet is one of the gayest things I've seen. The color-coded shirts, the rows and rows of shoes, the way you keep a padlock on it so nobody disturbs the perfection...sometimes I feel like I need to be listening to a Lady Gaga song just to walk in there."

"So I'm anal-retentive. So what?"

"And now you're 'anal' in an entirely different sense..."

He slaps me on the arm. Then he takes a short breath and pauses. "Listen, I..."

"Yeah?"

He's silent for a while. "Well," he says. "I have no shame about any of this – there's nothing wrong with anything gay – it's just...weird. I'm embarrassed that people were noticing things I never even noticed about *myself*. It's like suddenly finding out I was a blonde when I'd always thought I was a redhead."

"I get what you mean," I tell him. "Sometimes I feel like *none* of us know who we are at all, and we all just go

143

around lying all day until we figure out the truth…that's what life is, actually. A contest of who can lie the loudest, and therefore turn it into truth."

We hit a small hill that leads up to the wrecked bridge. In the end I actually *do* jump off the platform, but only under the agreement that Beau holds my hand as we do it. Finally he takes it, and then we step off the platform and fall twenty feet into ethereal white-blue waves…

On the way out of the park, we stop at a gas station. We both see the motel at the same time. ROOMS BY THE HOUR – 30$ PER, the sign says. He puts an arm on mine.

"I have to tell you something," he whispers needily.

"…Yes?"

"Keeping myself away from you was so fucking hard on that beach. I need you on my mouth, and I need it now. That's why I didn't want to take your hand. I was already uncomfortable."

My face goes numb, but I look around and remember we're in public, in a very conservative area, too. I shake my head. "No," I say. "That motel looks disgusting. It looks like venereal disease in a bottle, actually."

"*Please?*" he whines, his breath teasing the tip of my ear. "I like you, and it makes me want to…well, *be with you* all the time. And it would be such an…*experience…*"

I blush, then shake it off. "Yes, and that 'experience' would end in both of us getting chlamydia from the infected bed sheets. It's a no from me."

He leans in even closer and brushes against my ear, which I think he's already learned is the most surefire way to get me going. "But I want your fucking cock down my throat, Nathan Sykes. Can I have that?"

Every inch of my body ignites for him. How could I resist this? How could *anyone* resist this?

I glance over his shoulder at the motel, then back into his eyes. "So do you have thirty in cash, or will I have to use my card? I'm afraid to say I'm fresh out of bills…"

~

Within fifteen minutes we're entering a (surprisingly clean) room in the Isle of Palms Motel. I toss our key onto the desk and get ready to ask him what he wants to do next, and then-

Bam. I feel hands pushing me back, and before I can process anything, he slams me against the wall, buffering the impact with his forearm at the small of my back.

"Fuck," he breathes as he leans in. "I've been wanting to do this all day…"

And then he kisses me so hard, my vision goes out.

When I return to the present, I open my eyes and stare into his.

"That was the hottest thing you've ever done," I whisper.

"What can I say? Ugh, just stare at me. My eyes have missed you."

"Yeah, well, my tongue missed you, too. Now get on the bed."

The mattress is shockingly clean and comfortable, too. Soon we're both naked, chest to chest, nose to nose, dick to dick.

"Gimme this cock," he says from under me, planting a kiss on my forehead.

"Fine, but let me suck yours, first. I'm already craving that pre-cum, and I-"

"How about we do it both, then, together?"

"Huh?"

He reaches down, grabs me by the torso, and slowly swivels me all the way around so that he has access to my cock, and I have access to his, too. A regular sixty-nine…

"Oh…" I say, but he's already taken me all the way to the root. *Shit*, at this angle he can take *all* of me, and I lean my head back and moan. But then I feel my balls slapping against his forehead and remember it's time for me to get to work, too.

I swallow him up, making him grunt. Oh, Jesus – in this position, I can taste him while he sucks me, and it's almost too good to be real. I could do this forever, actually…

145

"Ugh, suck that dick," I say as I take a pause and watch. "Yes, just like that."

He kisses his way up to my balls, then my inner legs – which gives me an idea. We just went swimming, so I know he's clean – can I lick his hole?

I close my eyes, crane my neck forward, stick out my tongue, and make contact. Shit, he's so soft and smooth, and he tastes like skin and water and sugar. My cock getting even harder, I thrust my hips up and down to shove my dick down his throat, and start rolling my tongue in circles around his hole.

He spits out my cock, tilts his head sideways, and lets out the loudest moan I've heard yet.

"How does it feel?" I ask.

"It's...it's like...fuck...you need to feel this, too. It's heaven."

I lift up my body to give him a better angle, and as I return to licking him, he digs his face into my ass. Oh, Jesus...

From this angle, it feels like nothing I've ever experienced before. Now I understand why he had to stop sucking me and moan – it's like an angel from heaven is licking a spot I never even knew I had. (Just a really slutty angel.) Is this why girls could only ever orgasm while I ate them out? Is this what it felt like?

I stick my tongue further into his hole as he sucks mine. *Shiiiit*...his tongue is like a prickly-tickly-feathery tease down there, and I still can't quite get used to how it feels.

Suddenly I want every inch of him against me – in fact, stepping into his body right now wouldn't be enough contact. I reach my hands around his torso and press him to me so that our entire bodies are touching as we lick each other. I don't know who's moaning louder – me, or him. If anything it's like a glorious duet, each of us making sounds for each other while we please the other one. He does a funny little circular rolling thing around my hole and then plunges his tongue into me, and that does it – I reach down and grip my cock just as it pulses and throbs with the hardest orgasm I've probably ever had.

"Yes, dude," he says he sits up and starts licking up what cum he can reach on his upper chest. "Make that dick come for me."

That sends me totally over the edge, and I come for probably fifteen more seconds as he slurps up every ounce of my liquid he can. When I'm finally spent, he flips himself out from under me and jacks himself off onto my back, and I rub his nipples and kiss his waist to help him along. Finally he grunts once and then squirts all over my sweaty skin, mixing our liquids together in the sexiest combination I've ever imagined.

He collapses down next to me, and for a few minutes we just catch our breaths and stare up at the ceiling.

"Fuck," he says soon.

"I know."

"That was…"

"I know."

We just lay there, trying to breathe. Then I look over and say the thing that's really on my mind.

"Tomorrow is our last day together here. Do you realize that? Then it'll be back to the wedding shit, and after that, it's back to Charleston…"

"Ugh. I know. You don't have to tell me."

"Fuck my life…"

"How are we ever going to stop this?" he asks soon. "How am I ever going to go back to girls? Honestly, that would be like going back to ham sandwiches after trying filet mignon."

"I don't know. Do…do you at least feel any less awkward now, by the way? About the fact that I am…you know…"

"A dude? And also my best friend? And also my lover?"

I nod.

"I mean, I don't feel *bad* about it. I don't feel *good* about it, either. That part is just kind of…inconsequential? The friendship thing is mostly the sticking point for me, I guess."

"I know, I know, you don't have to tell me that, either," I groan.

"But don't get me wrong. I'm still having the time of my life."

"So am I," I say as I smile into his eyes.

"Be careful, though," he whispers, smirking.

"Why?"

"Because I wasn't supposed to like you, but if you keep licking my hole like that, we may have to re-negotiate the terms of that pact – *for good*."

~

When we head out of the parking lot and start back for Key West, he rests his hand on my leg. And this time, he doesn't move it an inch the whole way home. He is growing more comfortable with me now, and it feels like Hawaii after decades of January. Every moment is such a sweet, special kind of torture.

This is happening, I keep thinking to myself. It is really happening, because he is *letting* it happen. All we have to do now is keep the ball rolling...

As there's no roof above us, I watch the dying sun the whole way back to the hotel. Soon it's totally dark, and the sky is giving us the most dazzling star-show I've ever seen. Key West is at the end of a long, isolated island chain, and the sky here is so black, the stars are the brightest I've ever seen in my life. You can even see the stripe of the Milky Way running down the middle of the heavens – for a minute I can't even take my eyes away.

"Would you look at that?" I ask him, but by the tone of his response I can tell his face is not turned upward.

"No. I have enough to look at, and those stars could never hold a candle to it."

I look down. He's staring at me.

"Beau?" I ask breathlessly, caught in this gorgeous moment.

"Yeah?"

"Whatever happens when we leave, please know I wanted you since the first day. The first moment, really. I know that now."

He smiles appreciatively and just kisses my hand. But even as we return the car and start walking back to the hotel, the cranks in my mind won't stop turning.

The weird thing is, I never *wanted* to fall for Beau Lindemann. I really didn't. Sure, I wanted to taste his cum and squeeze his ass and choke on his dick all day, but *love*? The fluttery, teenager-y bullshit that Katy Perry talks about in her pop songs? No. That was never on my mind. For one, it would've changed everything I ever thought about my identity, and also, our friendship might never come back from that. You can't go from friends to more-than-friends and then back to friends again. You just can't. It's either this-or-that, forever-or-nothing. I've tried to maintain enough chilly, awkward relationships with former flings to know that fact down to my bones.

But still, some forces are non-negotiable. They move in and take over, and soon you are a prisoner to their intentions. And on a weekday evening in Key West, I do the unthinkable:

I start to fall, to really fall, for Beau Lindemann, my best friend in the world.

Beau Lindemann

We wake up together, and the next day is slow and easy and comfortable. It feels like French Toast, if that makes any sense at all – it's the kind of day that warms you up from the inside out. We mostly sit at the resort pool drinking a beer or two in the sun, both dreading the fact that this will be our last night alone together, but happy and grateful at the same time – and also sick with the knowledge that the wedding will be the last hours we spend in this paradise together before we have to return home.

Before three we head back to the room to shower and wash off the salt from the ocean. Nate's tanner than he's been in years, and from the moment he de-clothes, I can't take my eyes off him. How was it that I was able to be around this body for so long without seeing the beauty in his every square inch?

He showers alone, then gets dressed. When I pee and walk back into the room, my Nate is just staring at me, waiting.

"So. It's just about wedding day," he says.

"It is."

"What's with the weird look?"

"Nothing. No reason. Hey, would you be my date, by the way?" I joke. "I don't know of many single girls on the island who would be in a position to come with me…"

His eyes twinkle in a quiet way. "Sure. Only with you, though. Nobody else."

By late afternoon, though, I'm getting restless. I feel like I do when I'm hungry and become a rage-a-holic, so I eat a big early dinner, but it doesn't help. There's just something I can't shake off.

This evening is the last "bonding session" for the wedding guests before the big day – a final volleyball game on the beach. We're separated into two groups, and Lane looks directly at Nathan and me and then splits us up. I don't even want to think about why, so I head under the net and take up a position across from Nate. My Nate…even when I'm annoyed with him, he's still so sexy…

150

Maybe a little *too* sexy, actually. Without thinking he peels off his white shirt and tosses it onto the grass, and I catch not one, not two, but *three* girls looking at him like he's a human sex toy. And he is – he's just *mine*. I know he's hot, but why does he have to show it off like that? And sure, I know he doesn't know how hot he is, because of an awkward phase in his middle school years that damaged his self-esteem – but I still hate that all these other bitches get to stare at him, too. That should be *my* duty.

"Your serve," Lane says, tossing the ball at me so hard, it hits me on the shoulder. I roll my eyes and pick it up, and then I give Nate one evil look and then spike it – directly into his face.

"Fuck!" he shouts as it hits him in the cheek, spinning around, as the same girls blush and laugh at him. I don't feel bad, though. A volleyball isn't going to kill him, and he needs to know what I think about him putting on a strip-show for all these girls, who are single, tipsy, and on a beach vacation. Doesn't he know what he's doing?

Because of my foul, the serve is given to the other team – and Nate offers to do it. As I watch, he marches to the corner of the sand court, stares at me, and then spikes it so hard it zooms inches over the net – and hits me right in the balls.

"*Goddamn it,*" I pant, as I bend over and get the bizarre sensation that a train has slammed into the bottom half of my body. If you've never gotten a testicle injury, I hope you never do, because it feels something like a 50/50 mix between a sharp, stabbing pain and a dull, but still desperate, ache deep in your abdomen. You get an instant case of nausea, too, and I'm hunched over on the grass by the time I start listening again.

"You guys are gonna fucking kill each other," Harrison says as he grabs the ball and gets ready to serve. "Nate and Beau, take a hike and go fight each other or something, you're annoying us."

Nate stomps away, and when I can stand again, I start limping back to the room. As I get closer I start to take stock of my thoughts.

I love Natie – I know that now. But I've *always* loved him. How do I love him *today*? I will probably always have my mother's homophobia hanging over my head, and I'll probably *never* fully get over that whole thing. Is that what's holding me back, making me angry? Or is it the world in general? Or is it nothing at all, and I'm just creating problems in my own head, as usual?

The thing I keep coming back to is when I cried, when we were discussing my mom back on the kayak. I don't even know if he noticed, because I kept my face angled away. But maybe that's the issue – maybe I am disgusted that I let myself get vulnerable with him. Because he's always the person I let down my guard in front of, but that was just in the context of a friendship. He was the person who got me through my mom's death, actually. He was just there for me in ways nobody else was. To shift that perspective into a different frame, to risk putting it all on the line and showing him who I really am, but in the guise of a relationship – I still don't know if I can do that. And the prospect of losing the friendship in the first place still hangs over all this like low clouds in the distance at a barbecue.

It's all so stressful…if only I could find a new release, a new vent for this steam…

"Hey, Natie," I say that night, as we watch CNN. "I like this. I really do. Don't get me wrong. But…"

He pauses and looks over. "*But?*"

"Hold on. I was thinking about the kayak thing, and…how do we know this is a permanent thing? Like, for instance – say I wake up tomorrow wanting vagina. Or what if *you* wake up tomorrow wanting it?"

"Um," he frowns. "I wasn't thinking about tomorrow yet. Why is it so hard to live moment by moment? You'll drive yourself crazy if you live in the future."

"You know exactly what I'm saying, Nate."

He considers this for a moment, then starts chewing on his bottom lip. "Well…maybe you do still want a woman. But we never said that wasn't allowed in our agreement."

"What?"

"What we said was that you could fuck anyone you wanted, just as long as the other party knew about it. And we never said…"

"Yes?"

"We never said anything about *threesomes*."

My breath hitches. "Keep going."

"Well, maybe you want a woman already. That's fine. We never ruled that out. Maybe that's what we need – to explore some things. Do you know anyone who would be down to…well, hook up with two guys at once? Or maybe just watch us?"

I blush, look away, and nod. "*Actually*, yes. The chick I brought home the other night – she was a divorcé, she seemed a little lonely, and down for anything. And I mean *anything*. We can see if she's still staying at the hotel?"

He swallows. "Sure."

But does he really want this, or is he just pulling this out of a hat to keep me interested?

"You *really* want to do this?" I ask him soon, just to make sure. He smiles a little.

"I mean, why not? At least we'll be able to monitor our reactions, and decide how much we miss the whole 'being straight' thing. And besides," he says more seriously. "I don't think you understand that I would do *anything* in the world to find a way to make this work, Beau-Beau. And at least she's hot, right?"

And that does it. We put on our nicest outfits that weren't reserved for the wedding, drink some champagne to get loosened up, and then head to the dark, fancy hotel bar overlooking the pool.

At first I'm disappointed – it's the same business-y, middle-aged crowd as before, all murmuring to each other over glasses of wine and plates of peanuts. For a few minutes I think our plan has been dashed – *until* Nate nudges the back of my arm.

"Hey. I think that's her, over there, in the black. Isn't it?"

153

I catch the eyes of someone down the bar, and sure enough, I recognize her. And my memory from that night wasn't lying – she's pretty hot, too.

So I swallow the rest of my beer, set my eyes on her, and start for the empty seat next to her.

This should be interesting…

Birdie Lang

At first it feels like a dream. A particularly slutty dream, at that. I mean, what are the odds? Not only one hot, younger guy wants to hook up with me, but *two* of them do? Not only one tall, lean dude who looks like he just stepped off the set of a teen drama on the CW wants to fuck me, but a *double package* of them do?

I came to this place as a sort of last resort to save my sanity. My (soon-to-be) ex-husband's family held a timeshare in one of the resort's townhouses at the edge of the property, and when I saw that the final papers were about to go through, I jumped at the chance to stay here (and spend some of his money) before I officially become a divorced woman. And why not? Lord knows Jeffrey deserved it. I could take a million dollars from him and still not come close to getting the revenge I am owed, actually. But, ugh, don't even let me go there, I'm trying not to sound like a Bitter Betty and bring up the whole thing every five seconds, like many of my divorced friends who can clear out a room with their ranting and raving as soon as someone brings up the subject of their former spouses…

But pretty quickly I realized I was bored. I could only sit by a pool with a Miller Lite and Us Weekly for so long before I wanted to pull my hair out. All I was doing was thinking about my ex, revisiting the past, getting sucked back down memory lane. So I guess that's what led to me coming to a bar tonight. To sit here. Alone. Drinking profusely. Until Beau, from the other night, appeared again to ask for a redo.

First he apologized, and said he just wasn't on his game the other night. I can understand that – I haven't been on my own game in years. After a drink or two, though, it became clear what he *really* wanted. He couldn't stop making eyes at his little friend across the bar, and after ten or fifteen minutes he got to the point: they wanted to fool around with a "chick," as he called me. Now, listen here: I am thirty-four years old. I spent the last twelve years playing servant to a worthless piece of shit who treated me like his executive assistant and paid me in cold stares and emotional distance. So if two hot young guys

155

approach me and ask me for a good time, I would be fucking *crazy* not to say yes and see what happened, right? They look like two gay porn stars – which I do watch sometimes, by the way. But what do I have to lose? I've spent the last decade saying no to my own happiness, and to everything else the world had to offer me. Why not start changing that?

I roll with it. Beau invites the boy over, and he's cute and bashful and has an ass that could strangle someone. There's a weird electricity between us all, and they both keep glancing at each other, and then me, and giggling and looking away again. Finally I suggest we all order a tequila shot and then head back to their room. Whatever's about to happen, I want to be good and drunk for it. This would be too weird to process if I were anything less than tipsy.

But at the same time, I don't care if I'm making a mistake. It just feels good to be putting my hand on the button of fate in the first place.

We stumble back to the room, laughing like kids. (Oh wait, they *are* kids. Oops.) Beau opens the door and then I'm looking around at a large suite that smells like aftershave and sex. They really are together, aren't they?

Before I can even get my bearings, they start making out, but in the desperate, passionate way that two people who love each other make out. It's fucking sexy, to be honest. As I watch from the side of the bed, I can't decide who's hotter – Beau, for his rugged-ness, or the blonde, for the way he looks like he just stepped off the campus of a prep school. It's one of the hottest things I've ever seen in person, and not just in some video. But when the blonde drops to his knees and starts hungrily reaching at the brunette's belt, I clear my throat.

"Um, excuse me, gentleman – *why* was I called in here, again?"

"Oh," the blonde says sheepishly. "Sorry."

Beau slides onto the bed and kisses me. It's gentle, polite, and a bit boring – so I wrap my arm around his head. He moans into my mouth, and I look down and realize the blonde has whipped Beau's dick out of his pants and is sucking on it like there's no tomorrow.

Okay, then. This is certainly new.

Then I remind myself of what I'd be doing if I'd stayed back in my townhouse – I'd be drinking, by myself, yet again. I'd might as well try to enjoy this while it lasts, right? If nothing else, it'll be a story to tell my girlfriends when I get back to Toronto. Or maybe not tell them at all, actually…

Powered by the tequila, I undo my shirt and then slide out of my skirt, too. The blonde pushes aside my panties and starts teasing me, but I rock my hips into his face to tell him to go full steam ahead. And he does. Right now I just need to feel the touch of someone, anyone at all…

He's very good at this – surprisingly good, actually. Many men think eating a woman out is like a hot-dog-eating contest, where you demolish a vagina with your mouth and expect the woman to like it. But he's just the right mix of delicate and passionate. I lean back and get lost in the feathery, ticklish feeling…damn, he's good…

He moans, and I look up and realize Beau has gotten behind him, his muscled chest shining in the faint moonlight. He's about to fuck the blonde, doggy-style, while he eats me out…

"Can you eat that pussy while I fuck you from behind?" Beau asks.

"Yes," the blonde moans.

"Louder!"

"Yes, please!"

Boom. The blonde cries out as Beau enters him, then starts eating me more hungrily in-between his moaning. I can't say this isn't the hottest – and sluttiest – thing I've ever done, and seen, too. It doesn't even feel like I'm seeing it, actually – it feels like I'm watching the scene in a porno.

I hear myself moaning and sighing as the blonde slips a finger into me and licks my clit simultaneously. He motions his finger inside me, which is the tried-and-true way to hit the G spot of most women. My whole body clenches in reaction, and

I gasp. *Shit*, how did he know that? How does he know my body so well?

He licks, licks, licks, and soon I'm losing focus and the pressure is building in my core and I know I'm going to orgasm. That's right, I haven't orgasm'd by my husband's hand in probably seven or eight years, and yet here I am, about to come due to this twelve-year-old. (Obviously he's not twelve, but compared to me he might as well be. I practically feel like a babysitter right now.)

"Do you like that?" Beau asks, slapping the blonde's ass as he mounts him from behind. "I said, do you like it?"

"Yes, I do," the blonde says into my pussy as he pauses and closes his eyes. Then it's back to me again, and he pushes his finger in deeper and closes his lips around my clit. I cry out as my body convulses and rocks back, and he moans louder than ever as Beau fucks him harder and harder until…

Liftoff. I clench my core one more time, and then my body tumbles into a cascading world of twitch-y ecstasy. The bubbles and the lightness take over, and I yelp a few times as the orgasm explodes in me. Beau surges his hips forward one more time and then comes, and the blonde falls onto his side and does the same after only a few pumps of his dick.

Holy shit…all three of us just came, at almost the same time…

What kind of wild sorcery is going on here?

Ten awkward minutes later I've cleaned myself up in their messy bathroom. I turn back into the room and then stop – they're on the bed together, shoulder-to-shoulder, touching each other's hair and whispering about something. For a second I just smile and watch, my eyes prickling with tears in the corner. *Awwww.* More than anything I miss having that person. I miss someone loving me enough to touch me for no reason at all, I miss someone being so overcome for me, they want to brush my hair out of my eyes all day. I didn't find that in Jeffrey – that much is clear now. But by God, I will find it again. Or I will die trying.

I turn for the door and leave them to their canoodling. They deserve it. They don't ask for my phone number, and I don't give it to them, either. I know what I was for them tonight – a guest star, and that's fine. I'm okay with that. I've got a lot of shit to figure out before I'm comfortable becoming a starring player in someone else's show. And besides, from the way they kissed and sucked each other, it was clear they're interested in the same sex more than they'd ever be interested in me...

I take one last look at them, then head down the hall and listen to the door close behind me. Some things, I'm starting to learn after thirty-four years on this stupid frustrating planet, are just better left in the past.

Oh, and just for the record: I *will* be filing away every single detail from tonight into my memory, though, just for lonely nights in the future when the porn isn't doing it for me.

the edge
from the diary of Nathan Sykes

I used to feel *so small*
and now
I am your Taj Mahal

I used to wonder if anyone *really cared*
and tonight
I stand safely in your inferno

but honey,
now is not forever

and tonight
is not always

and I'm still on the edge

and soon
we've gotta be strong enough
to face the fire
of a world
that might not know what to do with us

so now I'm
standing at the end of that dock
we used to fish on, with your mother
back when she was alive

but I'm alone
and I'm waiting for you

and now I'm standing
at the edge of the world
wondering
are you going to take my hand?

because if you don't,
well...

I don't even know how to finish that sentence

I will never be strong enough to tell you this in real life,
but baby
you are the thing
that puts the air
into my lungs

and without that
I will just be *breathless*

Nathan Sykes

The actual wedding is being held back at the Hemingway House, in a beautiful little veranda near the mansion, in a corner of the garden. It probably cost a fortune, but oh well – it's not my money. When we show up late in the afternoon, the last tourists are being ushered out, and House employees are busy swathing everything in shades of cream and blush and buttery-yellow. The beauty of it alone murders me a thousand times. If I have to say goodbye to him, I don't want this to happen at all. Why couldn't our last night have been ugly and un-magical? Oh well. Fate has always been cruel. We are having One More Perfect Night, and then I might have to close off this part of my life forever...

After Birdie left last night, Beau took me by the chin and told me something. "You know how a slice of lime makes a vodka soda even better, but it's still great without the lime?" he asked me, and I nodded. "That's how that threesome was just now. It was fun, and watching you eat her was hot as fuck, but you're good enough, and I think you always could be."

But still that offered me no absolution, no certainty. When I returned from my walk on the beach with my black coffee earlier, he appeared from the bathroom looking absolutely breathtaking in a dark blue suit and skinny black tie, his tanned face and his messy hair making him look like a beach-ier version of a JCrew model. From the moment we walked down into the lobby, my brain was a senseless jumble of nerves – I was nervous and terrified and exhilarated all at the same time. I knew I was a goner. He'd taken me away – his eyes had transported me.

But was *he* a goner, too? In the same way I am? Because as well as I know him, his innermost thoughts are still mysteries to me, and the clock is ticking away every moment. Sweet words are one thing, but what is in his heart?

The wedding setup is gorgeous and looks like it probably cost a hundred thousand dollars – but then again, considering my circle, it probably did. Beside the mansion and the wedding gazebo is a massive, lit-up tent, with modern chandeliers hanging above a glossy bar in the center of the space. I can't wait to get drunk, but first we have to sit through the actual service. For the first time I am saddened by a wedding – they seem so perfect together, so natural, that soon I start to want this for myself, too. Will I ever get it, though? Or am I doomed to a lifetime of...grey?

I know I agreed to have my way with Beau Lindemann's body this week. The problem is, I think I started looking past that body, and fell for the heart at the center of it instead.

Once it's all said and done, we all rush into the tent to begin the after party, and the DJ starts spinning hip-hop songs from 2007 designed to make your oldest aunt get up and dance. The scene is pristine and pastel and perfect and a wretched explosion from hell, too. It's likely the last time I'll be with him like this, trapped in a paradise nobody knows about – we have to leave in the morning, and return to the real world, and deal with everything that entails.

The banter between my "friends" at the circular tables by the table is fairly routine, and nothing happens that raises any alarms – save for a few pretty terrible comments about the female cater waiters assembled by the bars. (If I keep paying attention to how awful these dudes are, I will be a skirt-burning feminist by the time I'm twenty-five, I swear.) After it all, though, I still can't believe I'm here. I can't believe I'm next to him, *here* with him, in so many more ways than one. Honestly I thought I was done before this – done with love, at least. Life chipped away at me like a sculptor at a block of stone, but it didn't make me a masterpiece. It made me a mess. People took and took and took from me until only darkness was left.

But here is Beau...

Except not anymore. Beau disappears to the bathroom, and then doesn't come back. I'm just starting to worry about him when I get a text that stops my heart.

Boy. Meet me in the bathrooms. The fancy one, in that big white building. You'll find it.

Why?

The response comes almost immediately: **Because sitting next to you without being able to touch you was torture, and I want my ass fucked before we leave Key West. Can you do that for me?**

I get up before I can stop myself. A public hookup, here, surrounded by these people, would be the most reckless thing we've ever done, but Lord knows we won't be able to stop ourselves, anyway...

Beau Lindemann

As the post-sunset wind peppers the air flowing into the Hemingway House courtyard with coconut and wet sand and suntan lotion, I think about one word: *curious*.

Curious was how I started this trip, but it's not how I want to end it anymore. I want to be sure, I want to be surefooted as a running back plowing down a football field. Talking to Birdie last night, listening to her divorce story and watching the sadness in her eyes, really got me thinking. So many people go through life listless and unfulfilled and curious. Curious about where they'd be if they'd taken that leap and asked for that promotion, or taken that chance and made that move to Denver. Curious about what would've happened if they'd hugged their mom the last time they'd seen each other before she died. Curious about whether they would've ended up happy if they would've walked back to the house of their first love in the pouring rain and laid out the truth, instead of letting it go and letting their love fade into the background like most other love does.

But not me.

Curious is how I feel now – I want to explore how I feel about Nate, to turn over my feelings like stones and figure out what's under each one. Because this wouldn't fit into my life. Could I make this work back in Charleston, where the "bro code" rules and where men are expected to act in a certain way, dress a certain way, live a certain life? I don't know. Running around on vacation with him and living a life with him back home are going to be two *very* different things. But then again, what choice do we have? Walking away at this point is just not an option. So I want to explore this. I'm sure of it now.

Curiosity is what brought me to him that first night in the Jacuzzi, and curiosity is keeping me here. (Yes, I knew he would be naked in that spa, and yes, I think on some level I was daring myself to follow him.) But I don't want to become Birdie. I don't want to spend the rest of my life being curious. Curious about what would've happened if we'd made it work, curious about what could've been if I'd just been strong enough to be myself…

Curiosity is also what led me to dive into Nate's diary earlier today while he went to the lobby to ask about check-out services. Yes, that's right: I took the chance to grab the little notebook and read what he's been writing, and I was blown away. (I swear it started as an accident – I was just tidying up the bedside table area, and then I saw the little book, and…oh, well. Sue me.) But every night, every single night, he's been writing about me. I'll never be able to tell him how much it meant to me, because *he's* the wordsmith here – not me. But I think I want to keep reading those poems forever. To see myself through his eyes, to see myself as someone worth all that love…well, I don't have the words. They fail me.

So taking the poems into account, I am making a pre-emptive strike against the curiosity, the regret, the what-ifs. I don't know if I'll be good at being with him. I don't know if we'll be perfect together in a world that still doesn't quite know what to do with gay people, as he put it. But I do know I want to figure it out. I want to try. I cannot, and do not want to, see myself with anyone else right now. And the sex – oh, God, the sex. I would probably be happy to slurp up his dick every night for a very, very long time.

In fact, I want it right now. His poems made me crave him more than ever, but we didn't have time. So that's why I just came here and called him to this restroom…

If you asked me a few days ago, I would've said that maybe we should just stay friends, and hook up on the down low. Shit, I know how our world treats gay and bisexual men, and it isn't pretty. It isn't pretty at all, actually. Even in places where gays aren't really *rejected* outright, they're still kind of just tolerated, and never allowed to forget how different they are.

But even the thought of parting ways with him makes a shudder run down my leg. And as I wait for him to find me, memories wrap around me like tendrils of ivy, lighting me up from the inside out. Yes, *yes*: I love him. I love Nathan Sykes. I mean, obviously I do. And *did*. When he flipped his motorbike

166

in high school and almost broke his leg, I remember I felt like I was drowning until I ran up and realized he was alive. When my dad died, I remember how low I was, how I couldn't take a full breath of air into my lungs until I saw him and knew for sure that he would be there. And when he got really serious with Elizabeth last year, a strange twinge of something angry and possessive used to tug at my stomach. I never liked her at all, I never wanted her around, and maybe I know why – maybe I wanted to *be* her. Maybe my fear was just putting wool over my eyes and closing me off to the possibilities of what could be.

But maybe *I* want to be the one holding his hand. Maybe I want to be the one going on fro-yo dates with him, laughing at memes in the corner with him. Maybe I wanted to be his best friend and the one who hears him cry out in the moonlight while we lose each other in the passion, too. Maybe I want to be the one who dies and fades away if he chooses someone else and does all of those things with them instead. Because love is not conditional, regardless of its form at any given moment. Who would I be without Nathan Sykes? I would be nobody. I would be a negative integer. He's inside me, holding me up, holding me together – he is like my bones.

So maybe I want to be the one he loves. Yesterday, now, tomorrow. And maybe I want it to start tonight.

He just has to find me first…

Nathan Sykes

"What are we doing?" I ask when I find Beau in the large "family changing room" that is separate from the other bathrooms. It smells like disinfectant and salt water, but it's spotless. He can't possibly want this – he can't possibly want me to make love to him here. Right?

But before I can even say more, he silences me with a deep, desperate kiss. It makes me feel...alive, in the simplest way.

"Well," I say when we come up for air. "I'll certainly take that for a greeting."

"Shut up," he whispers with a smile. "Can you please fuck my ass?"

"Um..."

"No hesitation. Please do it. Something happened, nothing bad, but I...I want to feel you. I want to fuck, and then talk – but definitely fuck first."

"You're sure?"

He pulls me so close I feel his breath on my chin. "Yes. I wanna feel my man inside me."

Okay, then.

"Do you have...?"

"Condoms and lube? Yep. In my pocket. Now bend me over the sink and fuck me."

That's all the insistence I need. Latching the door, I lick my lips and turn back to him.

"Fuck," he says.

"What?"

"That face – make it when you fuck me, okay?

"You got it," I say as I drop to my knees and undo his belt. "Now let's get you ready by sucking-"

"No," he says. "Just pull my pants to the bottom of my ass so I can feel our suits rubbing together when you fuck me."

"Good idea, babe."

I caress his firm, round ass a bit as I wiggle his pants down so that they're just exposing his hole. Then I undo my own fly and take out my cock, which of course is already seeping with liquid. I take the tip and rub it against his hole.

"You ready, babe?" I ask once I'm in a condom and we're both lubed up. His eyes, which I can stare into via the mirror, are hungry and almost closed.

"Yes. Fuck me. I want this. I want it while we're both still here, still hidden…"

"Trust me, I know what you mean. And hold your breath in the beginning – it'll sting until I open you up. You close up down there after every session."

"Listen to you – an expert, already!"

"Yeah, yeah. Now get ready for me to fuck you, baby."

I press myself against his hole, take a breath, and – bingo. I slide in about an inch, and he cries out far louder than he should be in a place this public.

"Bad boy," I whisper against his ear. "I know my cock is in you, you've just gotta take it like a man."

"Like a *what*?"

"That was awkward – you know what I meant."

I return my attention to burying myself in his tight hole. Damn. Just being in him is making me ready to bust already – he's *that* tight. Now I understand why he wanted his first time (besides the absolutely drunken session of wrestle-sex) to be like this instead of some romantic, kiss-me-in-the-moonlight thing – it's *hot*.

It's making this aggressive, animalistic feeling rise in me to be fucking his ass like this, but I try to swallow it down to keep things at least a little romantic. He is ten times tighter and wetter than any female I've fucked, and just inserting myself an inch has me groaning. Fuck.

"Relax, baby," I say. "I can't get in there if you don't let me inside. This isn't like last time. I won't force my way in there when you clench up."

He closes his eyes and breathes. I retreat a little and then sink deeper, and *holy hell* – he feels even better around more of my cock. We were made for each other, actually. Inch by inch I ease myself in him, and soon we're moaning and sighing together.

"Fuck," I hear myself say. "This is so fucking tight. I love this."

"So do I," he pants. "I'm ready. Fuck me. Fuck me hard, Natie. My Natie."

I grunt into his ear, bite his earlobe, and thrust for the first time, pushing my body forward and shoving myself into him with all the force of almost twenty years of team sports. He leans back and cries out as I do it again.

"Fuck," he groans. I love that sound so much already. "Fuck *fuck*."

"You ready to take it for real now?"

His eyes pressed shut, he nods. "I'm ready."

I grab him by each hip, take a breath, and *boom*. Another thrust, another cry he is barely able to stifle. Drilling him, I lean back a little and reposition his lower body to get a better angle. It's almost like fucking a woman, except I have his big dick to play with while I fuck him – damn, once again, I can't believe we never did this before. I feel like we just wasted so many years of potential pleasure...

Lifting his pelvis, I slam my cock into his hole until I'm at the root of me, getting deeper than ever. He bites his finger so he won't scream, and then we lock eyes in the mirror.

"How does it feel for you?"

"Like heaven, baby. Keep fucking me."

"Yeah?"

"Yeah, my dude. *Please*."

Within seconds I'm fucking him so hard, his body is bouncing back with each thrust. It's so hard to control myself from busting, but suddenly I am distracted by a thought – how does it really feel for him right now? What's going on inside that head, and why did he ask me for this right *now*?

Beau Lindemann

I moan as he sinks into me deeper. "Ahhh, babe…"

"Nah," he says, wrapping a huge hand over my mouth as he nibbles at my ear. "Don't make a sound while I fuck you. We're in public. You'll get us into trouble, silly. Good boy. Now stay quiet while I fuck your lights out."

I adjust my body as I try to get used to how this feels. The other night, during our romantic little sex session, that was making love, and that was amazing – but this is *fucking*. I am getting *fucked* by him. And it feels just as good, just in a more raw, real, visceral way. I want him to invade me, I want him to fuck me and make me his own. Just thinking of that word alone makes me wet, literally makes me seep. Holy shit – suddenly it occurs to me that we could live together and use each other's holes every morning and night, *and* we could have each other's friendship at the same time and never get lonely – it would be like dating a woman, but without all the dysfunction, and with semen all over my face every night, to boot.

He pounds me harder and harder and harder. Just the concept of it is sexy and a bit daring and dangerous. I'm *getting it* from Nathan Sykes. He's *fucking me*. I'm his bitch right now. The moans he's making are due to me. His eyes rolling back into his skull – that's all me. To see the cause and effect of it, as I feel him inside me…it's weirdly intoxicating in a way I never experienced with a female. I thought I'd want slow, romantic sex for my first semi-sober encounter, but no – he makes me want to have manly, aggressive things done to me. I don't want to make love, I want him to fuck my living brains out.

"Fuck me," I say. "Fuck me harder."

And he does, both hands wrapped around my waist. For a moment I am taken away – this is just on another playing field. It's animalistic, primal, revolutionary, and I never want it to stop…

For the first time, we actually orgasm together, a stuttering, gasping little infinity that stretches out into the Key West night.

171

Oh, yes, I think when he finally pulls out of me and kisses my shoulder. This is what I came here for. And this is what I hope to *keep* getting after we head back to Charleston, too…

Soon he clears his throat and looks at me expectantly, making me jump with nerves. "So…you wanted to talk?"

Nathan Sykes

Beau takes a deep breath, pauses, and then says that all along, he just wanted to tell me I looked hot in this suit tonight.

"That's *all?*" I ask. He looks like he's lying, but I'm not totally sure.

"Um...yeah. That was all."

I'm not sure if I believe him, but oh, well...we both know we don't have much time to be separate from the party. So we return to the reception silently and, I am guessing, red-faced and messy-haired. I walk in first, and then he follows two minutes later, as we arranged. Sex just makes him look more gorgeous and perfect and heavenly and model-esque, and every second he is not under my tongue is a second I loathe. (Can you tell I'm falling in love? Ugh, I sound like a character in a Harlequin novel, even to myself.) As we return to the table and slip back into chit-chat with the few guests who aren't on the dance floor, I start to let my mind wander...straight into Beau-ville.

In physics, there is something called the multiverse theory. I read about it a few months ago, during my nightly nerdy time I enjoy after everyone else falls asleep. Anyway, the theory says that all decisions we make are both interconnected and independent, and that our lives contain a billion little potential universes that could be created if we make this decision or that decision – say, if I choose to fly to Puerto Rico instead of China, that trip to China still exists in an alternate universe somewhere, because I still went on that trip in my head before deciding against it. It's just imaginary, but it still exists. Our lives are a million different worlds inside a prism, all colored by the choices we make every single day. Our thoughts give off energy, and energy is matter, so dreams are real. Inside that prism, and inside my dreams, my grandmother is still alive with her quiet smile and her grey eyes, and she never chose to stop eating and die after my grandfather passed away, and she still loves me. She's still here in a way because I *want* her to be here, and my fantasies have inherent power. And also inside that prism, my first crush chose to like me back

173

instead of walking away, and she *didn't* leave me alone at the bus stop to cry in the searing sunlight while my friends laughed. I love to wander down those unexplored hallways in my daydreams sometimes, and live all those unlived lives...

But tonight a sense of urgency weighs on me like I've never felt before. Because I don't want Beau and I to exist only in the multiverse. I don't want us to be some beautiful but missed possibility that I dream about fifty years from now in my deathbed. I want our love to exist in real life. I want to love him in *this* universe. And I'm starting to realize I can't let him go until I chase that chance with everything in me.

Some people describe falling in love as being like finding a new favorite book, but falling in love with your best friend is like realizing your favorite book was on your shelf all along – you'd just shoved it there one day and forgotten about it. Before, my love for him lived hidden inside a million different little moments of 'friendship' – the time I got enraged upon seeing him on a date and left the theater for no reason at all, the time he broke his finger and I found myself on pins and needles for hours, worried sick about him. My love for him was there, it was just latent, waiting for the moment that would see it pounce out of the darkness and stake its claim.

And now, wrapped in light and thunderously announcing its own arrival via my heartbeat, my love is *here*. It is everywhere, actually. Now I've just got to find a way to carry it into the future, to make our love real in *this* life, instead of it being just another beautiful possibility buried in my own personal pile of what-ifs...

~

An hour before the reception's closing time, the guests are starting to stumble out of the gate and trickle home. My dude, who's gone off to pee, appears at the fountain looking curiously empty-eyed. I can't tell if he's sad or shocked or emotionally moved or...what?

"What's going on?" I ask him. "That was a long pee. I thought we were leaving. Where were you?"

174

"Nowhere," he says, and there's some weird kind of smile in his eyes. Then I realize it: he's wasted.

"Were you drinking alone?" I ask, and he burps and wipes his face.

"I don't know. Maybe."

"Why?"

Finally he faces me. "Because I...I'm scared, Nate. Lane saw us. Twice."

"*What?*"

"He just told me, after I left the bathroom. He saw us holding each other in the car, too, and you never told me. That's why I just took a bunch of shots."

First I waver a little. Then I dig a heel into the ground and roll my eyes. "Oh, great, we're back there?" I ask, trying to seem calm. "Awesome. Just awesome."

He looks away, indignant. "It is awesome. Sex is awesome. So are Southern bigots."

I come closer. "Beau," I say. "What is this?"

"She called me a sissy," he said, his eyes screaming.

"What? Who did?"

"My mom, one of the last times I ever saw her, she called me a 'sissy' for not being able to hit a baseball in a certain way. That is one of the last memories I have of her, of her pushing me down and insulting me. I was staying with my dad all the next week, so I hadn't even seen her alive much before I found her. That's what I've had to live with all this time. That's why I pull away sometimes when I get close to people...but trust me, Natie, I like you so much. I like you so much it terrifies me...I just don't want to be a letdown...like I was to my mom..."

I try to respond, but just then, the worst person in the world appears – Lane Bryant, that deep-fried Pillsbury Doughboy himself. *Again*. He's waddling past in his khakis and his navy blazer, tumbler full of whiskey in hand as he talks shit into his phone, as always. At first I am positive he is not going to notice us – and then he does. Of course.

He stops mid-sentence.

175

"Hey, what are you two lovebirds doing?" he asks, hanging up. "I guess all the chatter is true. Get back to the wedding, this isn't a date night for y'all."

"We'll be there soon," says Beau is low, cool voice. Lane steps forward, smiling with a grin that is so slimy, so *gross*, I just want to kick him right then and there.

"What's that?" he asks in a condescending baby voice. "Aw, so it's not just a rumor – you two really are shackin' up! My eyes weren't deceiving me! So tell me, which one is catchin' and which is pitchin'?"

I halfway think Beau is going to grab me and walk away. I want him to just leave Lane to his own misery – because truthfully, that would be the best choice. He is trash, he is beneath us, and we don't need this in our lives.

Instead, Beau wipes his cheek and stands a little taller. "Actually, we switch off. We find it works better that way. And I like how it feels, too."

All the color leaves Lane's blotchy, ruddy face. In fact, he seems to shrink about three inches. If I weren't so nervous, I'd laugh.

"…What?" he asks, thrown. "I was just kidding – are you guys *really* – are you…"

"I guess it's up for you to decide," Beau smirks. "Unless the alcohol has already eaten all your brain cells, that is."

"Whatever," Lane says in a lower voice as he turns away. "Couple'a fags."

"Say that louder," I say after him, and Beau looks over at me with horrified eyes. Now I am the one mouthing off, but I can't help it – because people like this need to be fought. Nobody will ever be able to go back and stand up to Beau's mom and tell her how wrong she was, but here is a new chance – and it could be the thing that solidifies this thing between us.

But…shit, I'm also scared. Sure, Lane is a big, dumb oaf, but he's probably *two hundred pounds* of big dumb oaf – nobody ever messes with him, because he throws his weight around and fights dirty. There's no telling which way he'd go in a fight. But I don't care. I am murderous right now.

"I said, you're fags," he finally spits. "Not that I care, but you are. And regardless, whether you're diddling each other or not, you're still...*soft*. Always were."

My mouth opens. For some reason I don't think of *myself* then – I think of every single gay kid out there who's been under siege by someone like Lane, all the kids who were smaller and weaker and less brash than the pieces of shit who were taunting them.

"Lane, why are you such a fucking piece of shit?" I suddenly hear myself say. "Who poured piss in your Cheerios and made you so miserable? Say that Beau and I *did* suck each other all day – what in the fucking world would it have to do with you? How would it affect you or your dumb little life in any fucking way whatsoever?"

He doubles back, but then his eyes narrow. "You don't know who you're talking to."

"Oh, yeah, yeah, lemme guess," I say as I roll my eyes. "You're gonna tell me how rich and important you are, and how your shit smells like garden roses and..."

"No," he says flatly. "I was going to mention that my dad left my mom for a dude."

"Lane, you...*what*?"

"Our interior designer, Lance," he says inscrutably. "My dad left her for broke, and she's been struggling ever since. All because he wanted to go live with his boyfriend."

Well, I think to myself, this explains why he's such a miserable ape...

"Listen...sorry," I say soon. "And it sucks that they split up, but it has nothing to do with us, and what you think is going on here."

I see him look us up and down – *is it worth it?* he's wondering. Should he risk it, or should he walk away?

"I have no problem with it," he says, his face more red than usual. "Whatever it is. Just keep it private – nobody wants to see that shit. It's just not natural. Keep it to yourself."

He turns to leave, and a revolution boils in my blood unlike anything I have ever felt before. The other day I saw an article about whether we should "punch Nazis" – basically, a

Nazi-connected group was growing in prominence, and people were debating whether we should "respect" their free speech, or try to take them down since they were, you know...well, *Nazis*. But all at once I know there is no "respecting" bigotry – people like Lane want me to go away, hide, erase myself from the world. And for what? I know he's not a Nazi, but it still applies here. Am I going to let him put me in danger with his words and his attitude? Or am I...*not*?

"Say it again," I hear myself growl, pounding towards him. "I don't care who your dad is. Say that one more fucking time."

He turns around and smiles at me as condescendingly as he can. "Damn, Sykes, you're dramatic tonight, aren't you? Fine, I'll say it again – keep it away from me, whatever it is. I just don't want to see that faggot-y shit."

A burst of pure energy surges from the bottom of my left ankle, up through my torso, and explodes into my arm. Then it powers me to ball my fist, retreat one side of my body to draw leverage, and then – as Lane watches with disbelieving eyes – let my arm fly.

And then I do it.

I punch a bigot in the face.

Beau Lindemann

"*Shit*, Nathan!"

I run up and grab him by the shoulders as Lane lurches backward and falls to the ground. Sure, I love every minute of it, but you can't just *punch* people, either. When I turn Nathan to me, he's dazed and blank in the face, and I shake him a little. "Nate! You okay? What was that?"

"I...I think I just punched a Nazi," he says, still dazed.

"You...what? Nate, he's not a Nazi..."

But he doesn't care – he's still staring right through me. Lane, on the other hand, backs up against the wall and stares up at us.

"Freaks!" he says. "Losers. You'll regret this. My great-uncle's the best lawyer in Columbia!"

Suddenly something hits me – Lane is pissed, and he's just given us a perfect ransom to hold in exchange for our secret, too. He would be *humiliated* if everyone found out about his dad – there's no reason to be embarrassed, but clearly he would be. And of course, I would never actually "out" someone to the public – but then again, Lane doesn't know that.

"You fell onto the deck on a fishing excursion from the resort," I tell Lane as I walk over and lean in, "and you hit your head, and that's why you'll have a black eye in the morning."

"What?"

"This never happened. Tell anyone about it," I whisper into his ear, "and everyone at this wedding will know about your dad – and that's a bigot's worst nightmare, isn't it?"

He pauses, stares, and pouts. And with that, he finally scurries off. I turn back to Nathan and wrap an arm over his shoulder.

"Jesus. Your knuckle is already huge. Let's get you home, okay, big guy?"

"Um," he asks, finally coming back to me, mentally speaking. "Did I just...did I just *fight* someone?"

"I mean...kind of," I laugh. "It was pretty awesome, actually. I just think you're a little psychotic for punching a

179

little dipshit who would like nothing more than to send you to jail for assault – and tell everyone in the world about us, too. But we'll have to wait and see about all that…"

His shoulders fall. "Oh. I guess I didn't think about that. Sorry. Something just came over me – I can't even describe it. And shit, he's gonna tell people eventually, isn't he?"

"Probably," I nod. "Not now, because I threatened him, but eventually – yeah, he probably will."

"What're we gonna do, then?"

I rub his shoulder just like I did the other day in front of the mirror – but this time, I don't want to let go. "I mean…deal with it, I guess? God, you really sobered me up just then. I feel fine now. Maybe you should start a fight *every* time I get drunk…"

He still looks tense, and for a while we just walk alone in the darkness. Then he looks over and smiles. "Oh well. Let's head back for the bus, yeah?"

"You read my mind. Let's get out of here."

"Oh, and what were you going to tell me earlier?"

I swallow hard. "Um…"

"Um, *what*?"

"I'll tell you on the bus. Let's just get some privacy first."

Nathan Sykes

I follow Beau into the air-conditioned charter bus. Most of the guests either left early, too drunk to continue, or are still dancing. So we're largely alone as we take seats.

I rest my head against his seat, lulled into peacefulness by the hum of the idling engine. I can't believe how long today felt – it was one of the longest days of my life, actually. And soon I am drifting, drifting, drifting…

"Hey," Beau says soon, and it seems like he's nervous for some reason. "Do you remember the promise we made to each other when were in – like, probably the sixth grade?"

"The one in the tree?" I ask, and he nods.

"Yeah," he says. "I fell out of that tree, and you said you'd never leave me. You said you'd stay with me in the ambulance, and you did. 'You sing, I sing,' remember?"

"Of course. It was your birthday. I felt terrible you were going to miss your own party, and so I started to sing the birthday song, and your dad told me to shut up. But then you joined me, and I told you that every time you ever sing in the future, I'll sing, too. 'You sing, I sing.' I'll never forget it. God, such a crazy memory. Why do you ask?"

"Because I…I do want to keep that promise," he says. "Just…as your friend."

And my world shifts on its axis. "*What?*"

"Yeah. That's what I had to tell you. I just had to…be alone for it."

My head is spinning now, but I struggle to stay calm. "But I – I thought we were moving forward…I thought we were, well, *more* than friends now…"

He pauses. Takes a breath. And says this:

"Yeah. But I can't do this."

I lean back and do a double-take. "You…*what?*"

He looks away again. "I'm sorry. But this place isn't real. Key West isn't Charleston. I've decided this isn't going to work out in the real world."

I try to swallow, but I can't. My posture sways like my spine has disappeared. My stomach shrinks, then plummets. "Not...*real*? What? What do you even mean?"

"It's just not worth it," Beau says casually. "I was thinking, and maybe I want to get back with Megan, my ex. It would be so easy, you know? Not...complicated, like this."

My forehead becomes wet with sweat. My pulse races. It still doesn't make any sense. "Are you...are you *serious*?"

"Sure I am. I don't even really think we should talk when we get back to Charleston."

I feel like I'm dying. I can't process it, can't understand it, can't accept it. I guess there's nothing like the glancing blow of love to remind you of how breakable you really are, right?

And then just like that, he gets up to leave.

"Wait," I say. "Wait. You're really going?"

"I am. This is how it has to be. I'll call an Uber."

"But I...you're my best friend, and..."

"I'm sorry, Nate. I don't know what else to say."

I can't even form words. "Can I...can I kiss you on the cheek? Can I kiss you goodbye?"

Reluctantly, he leans forward, as if I am just an afterthought. I wrap my arms around him, trying to bottle his scent, trying to make this moment last forever...I can't believe this is goodbye...but then again, I can...

Everything has led to this. All of it, since the very first moment, was a mistake.

And just like that, it is over. All of it. We drive back home separately, and upon our return to Charleston it's like Key West never happened at all. He doesn't call. He doesn't even text. And soon...just as I dreaded, normality returns.

I try to settle back into my life, but there is no life to settle into. Weeks become months, and then Christmas comes, cold and lonely. Losing my best friend – as well as the person I loved – has dealt an unfixable blow to my life, it seems. I am learning more and more than I am not me anymore. All the memories I made with him by my side – they're not real anymore, because where did the other half of them go? The

182

hardest moment happens every single day, again and again – the hardest moment is when I think of one of our inside jokes, or see something that would be of interest of him, and then take out my phone and must remember, all over again, that he's not there anymore. He's there, of course; out in the world getting on with his life without me. He's just not there *for me*. He cut the cord. It's done. Ashes to ashes. Dust becomes dust. And that is the ultimate tragedy, that he is indeed out there, just not when it comes to *me*. Sometimes I think I'd rather he'd have died. At least I'd have a ghost to mourn – but how can I mourn someone who still breathes?

It's almost been a year when I get the letter in my family's mailbox. For the first few times, lately I'd recently started feeling alive again – once I found myself humming to a song as I walked, and another time I laughed at something. I actually laughed! My life is still nowhere close to normal, though, and my distress only grows as I read the letter, written in his sloppy handwriting:

Natie,

I've tried to write this letter over and over again, and every time I do, I stop. But this time I will finish. You need to know a few things, Nate.

The truth is that I was never going to be strong enough. I always knew. I felt it lurking in me during those seven days of heaven, those days I will remember for the rest of my life. But I was never going to be able to get over my mother's assumed disapproval, my nerves about how the world would accept us, my uncertainty over the future...

This would've happened anyway. Trust me on that one. So please don't be angry at me. Looking around now, at a world that seems to be going backwards if in any direction at all, confirms this. All I did was cut the cord sooner rather than later.

Oh, Natie, I miss you so much already. Don't ever think that's not the case. Sometimes, when I really really need you, I imagine we were born into a world that actually let us love each other instead of driving us apart in fear. I want you to take a moment and imagine that place with me, too, even if it never becomes reality. Just think: it's last year again, and I am standing on that beach behind the Waldorf. You walk out onto the sand and find me. I turn around and smile. And the waves never stop breaking, and the breeze never stops blowing...

Until that world happens, I do the only thing I can: I set you free. I only pray that one day, even if it happens far in the future, you will forgive me.

-Beau

I take the letter, seal it in a plastic box, put it under my bed, and do not touch it again for another eleven months. And the next time I do touch it, Beau Lindemann is someone's husband.

Beau Lindemann marries, of course, to one of the girls he was juggling before those halcyon days when we allowed ourselves to be together. After that I block him on every single social media account – seeing his posts come across my feed is like taking a knife to the heart, and so I learn to remove myself. I still follow his life with a sense of removed horror, though. There are occasional updates I find when I get drunk and let my mind wander onto Google – he had his children, naturally, two little brunette ones, and got a job at a big company that outsourced jobs to India or Bangladesh or somewhere. Really, he acquired the life we both knew he would always find. Key West was just a detour. A temporary one. And so was I.

Most of the time I am okay, because I have learned to tell myself I am okay until I believe myself. Mostly I just think of him. No matter how much time passes, that never changes. Even though *I* do change.

Is he happy? Is he proud? Is he...well, is he Beau, the same Beau he let himself be around me? More than anything in the world, I hope he's himself.

And I even though I pretend every day that I am okay, I am really not fine at all. The years speed by with increasing swiftness, and soon I am pulling grey hairs from around my temples. Several nights a week, I still close my eyes and watch him dance in the dawn of my memories. Where is he out there?

Who has he become? He will never know how often I still sail back to those times in my mind, revisit the days when we were together and the whole big bright daring world was ours. Does he still miss Key West? It never ended for me. But does he still think about when his smile was the only thing I saw, when I could reach down and feel firm ground under me? After all these years – well, decades, really – I'm still not over him. I'm still not over the fact that society wouldn't let us be together because we were both boys. His hands will never let me go, even if he's physically gone. A love like ours, I know now, sinks down deep and doesn't let go, and now all I can think about is when he was mine and I was his. When we were each other's, and my home was in his eyes. When the whole world was thrilling, when the only things we could see were the lights. When we were nirvana...

So one day in the late afternoon of my life, I sit down and write him something:

Dear Beau,

I was a wide-open prairie
fertile and strong and good and proud
and you treated me like a patch of dirt
in your rearview

and now

I've carried the burden of your departure for far too long
my back is so sore,
and my dreams
are so haunted

so this load, this baggage
I cast it off
and give it to you

because darling,

I enjoyed every moment I spent loving you
but I never deserved
all the sorrow you left me with

so take it on your back
and get going.
because I don't deserve to hold
all the anger you left me carrying

you know,
I used to think I was like an old sailor removed from the sea –
I would still think of you forever

but not if I can help it

so now I am freeing you
to be just as lost as I was
without you

because I was the best gift you never opened

and losing me
is about to become your greatest mistake
and my own
greatest triumph

I sit back, pleased with myself, as the memories sear my mind. And then I do what I knew I would do all along: I get up and throw the letter in the trash and get on with my life.

Some things, I know, are just better left unsaid.

I get the letter on a cold morning in March. It is halfway into the new century, and although much has changed, humans are still the same. I've moved into the assisted living home by now, and my favorite nurse, Michelle, drops the letter in my box with a big smile. I smile back and open it up, confused as to why someone's handwritten me a letter when nobody's done that in years – and then I see the Charleston return address and feel my heart sink.

Nathan,

I'm sorry for writing. I'm an old fool. But if you're reading this, I'm already gone. Life's funny that way – one day you're twenty-something years old under the moonlight with the great love of your life, and five minutes later you're being told the tumor in your lungs is going to take you in a few days, and you're far too old to qualify for a transplant. Before that happens, though, please know that you gave me the time of my life. I am so grateful.

It's also funny how, as you grow older, you think more about the things you didn't do than the things you actually did do. Nathan, I would give anything to roll back the clock, find myself with you back in Florida, and prevent myself from leaving. Walking away from you wrecked by whole life – I can admit that now. I knew it very early, actually, and just didn't know how to fix the mess I'd made.

In another world, we found a way to be together. Just not this one. Now, this is all I beg of you: please remember the best of me. Please remember who I was, not who I became. Again, I beg you. There's else I can do right now but beg.

I thank the universe for letting me smack into you, Nathan. If I could, old friend, I'd do it all again. And when I go, whether tonight or in five minutes or five days, know that I will go with your face in my mind. Nobody else's.

With all my greatest love,

- Beau Lindemann

Michelle, the nurse, appears at the door to my unit again as I sit there, slumped in my chair, sobbing silently. It would've meant the world to me for Beau to have said any of this when we were actually together, when the sun was still over our shoulders. But that's the thing about humans – they're always letting you down when you need them the most. But oh, well. A love that big can only be found once. Never again.

"Is everybody on?" Michelle asks. I look up at her and sniffle.

"What, now?"

"I said, is everybody on?"

As I stare up at her, her face blurs, and her voice changes. Then I hear it again: *is everybody on?*

But then I realize it's not her speaking at all – it's someone else.

It's a man.

~

I open my eyes and rub them. I'm back on a bus, in a seat next to Beau. But the *young* version of him. The real version. And the bus driver is calling out to see if everybody has returned to the bus.

I look over at Beau.

"Jesus, what's wrong?" he asks me. "You look like someone just died."

"Beau, what – what's going on?"

"What do you mean?"

"What year is it? How did we get here?"

He laughs a little. "Um. It's 2017, Natie. You punched Lane, we got on the bus, and you passed out. The driver stopped at the gas station and got into a conversation with the clerk that lasted forever. But we're leaving again now."

I feel my arm to make sure I'm awake. "We...we've been...hooking up, right? I didn't imagine all that, did I?"

He peers over his shoulder. "I mean, yeah, but I didn't know we were talking about it so loudly like this yet..."

Relief flows through me like cold water. Jesus, I know I have vivid dreams, but that one just took the cake...

I throw myself against his body, clutching him like I've never clutched him before. "Oh my God, Beau. I...I just dreamed you didn't want me. It was so vivid. You were so mean. You said we couldn't hang out anymore after we get

188

back to Charleston. And then we got old, and…and you were married, and…and…"

"Nate," he asks, concerned. "Are you okay? Why in the world would I ever do that? We're best friends."

Finally I try to get ahold of myself. "Yes," I gulp. "Okay. I know. I'm fine. Sorry. Dear God, that was just so real…"

He pats me on the head. "Looks like you're gonna have to get over your self-doubt. Enough anxiety dreams. You're my favorite person, Natie. Start believing it."

He wraps an arm around my shoulder and tries to pull me in. But the dream still hangs over me.

It was so real, and so disturbing. I would rather die right now than have that become my future. If I could use *this* moment, this one moment, to convince Beau to stay with me forever, what would I say?

I lean closer. And this time, *I* am the one who brings up our tree house promise, which he says he remembers. No more evasions. It is time for all of my truth. It is time for me to speak now.

"Well, the thing is…I want to keep that promise," I begin. "This might sound weird, so just…bear with me. But I want to see where this goes, Beau. Because I…I think I love you. I mean, obviously I did before, and I always have. But now I love you in the way…in the way beaches love sunrises, in the way TNT loves a spark. I think I loved you from the beginning, and I think I love you now, but in a different and better and bigger way, and I know I'll love you tomorrow, too. I always will."

His lips part. "You really *love* me? You really do? In…that way?"

Ugh. How can I say this? How can I say: *I dreamed about you in dreams I never even knew I was having, and you are the answer to prayers I never even knew I was making?*

How do I describe all of that without having him fill out a police report for stalking?

"I already knew I loved you, as my best friend," I say, the gentle hum of the bus providing background music. "But this week changed my life. Now I think I love you in…in ways I never even realized, in ways I can't even wait to start exploring, in ways that make me want to fall asleep with you and wake up with you and be around you every second, " I say with my eyes closed. Then I sigh, open them again, and wait for his response.

At the end of the day we are just two guys, abandoned by the girls we thought we'd once loved, alone at the end of the road together. But maybe we'd been alone for a reason – maybe we'd been waiting to strip away all the fear and admit we felt the same love inside. From two little kids in South Carolina to two men in a chain of islands in Florida – maybe everything had led to this. I'd been on a desperate search for happiness my whole life – in the form of women, partying, booze, whatever. But I'd been looking so hard, I'd failed to notice that the key to contentment was perhaps right in front of me all along.

"You know what? What the hell – I love you, too," he says, then he laughs into the darkness, and I feel lighter than oxygen. "I've been so fucking terrified so say it, but – I love you, too, Nate! I just needed to be budged into saying it. The stuff with my mom will nag at me, but fuck it, I'm an adult – I'll deal with it. But isn't that strange and wonderful to say? Oh, what a fucking world! *I love you!*"

He grips me harder and laughs into my shoulder. And suddenly I feel like I just won every race that was ever run, every lottery that was ever played, watched every sunrise and sunset that ever bloomed and died over this rock we call home.

He loves me. He really, really loves me. My best friend loves me. As more *than my best friend. And I love my best friend, too. Forever, maybe.*

I smile into his hair. I know the trip ends tomorrow, but we have *so* much time to explore what this is, to explore each other's souls, to travel and learn and read books and watch Netflix and try to build a life together in ways we never even imagined before. But he is worth the wait – and the risk, too. Because this could be *hard*. Our world is decades behind with this issue, and also, we know each other in a platonic way that could prove tricky to transform. But he's worth it. And the transformation is already happening, too – slowly, but it's happening. Already.

The bus rolls to a stop outside the dark hotel, and together we head to the front of the aisle and wait by the door. It's time.

"Fuck," he laughs soon, still sort of in disbelief. "How will we know how to act? What will we tell our families? Oh, we…"

"Beau," I say, shushing him. "Shh. I have you, and therefore I have everything. And fuck – if nothing else, we just found the biggest adventure of our lives, right?"

He nods as the door slides open with a whining sound. As we exit together, I take his hand. He lets me take it, too, and squeezes it in return.

And into the misty night we go, walking bravely but unsurely into a world of a million possible tomorrows…

May

June

July

August

September

I Lied
from the diary of Nathan Sykes

I have a confession to make.
I lied

in the twenty-or-so years I've been lucky enough to know you,
I've told more than a few untruths

like:

when we were eleven
and you accidentally kicked me on the trampoline
I said it didn't hurt
but my leg was throbbing like hell

and in high school, when you went to homecoming with that girl
I said I was having a great time
but every second of watching you with her
was a machete in my guts

and when I told myself I didn't love you
every single time –
those were lies, too

the other night I had a dream
starring God
and He told me
that the bravest thing anyone could ever do
is to be bold enough to love
in a world that just wants you to be afraid

and now I feel so bold
because I know

that you and I
were written in the stars

and meant to end up
in the same epilogue
together

still,
I know it's scary
and I know that sometimes
you don't know the boundaries
of this new kingdom between us

but you are my destiny
so darling,
pick up your pen
and let's keep writing this thing
forever

even when
we must
write our own way forward...

Five Weeks Before Halloween
Nathan Sykes

Spoiler alert: the world is not kind to all forms of love.

Seasons change. People change, too. They get older and soon they're not themselves anymore. Take my parents' love, for example. They are not divorced, but they barely live together, and when they are in the same room an icy silence suffocates everyone who is near. Or maybe Beau's parents' love – his mom drank and drank and drank because she was left alone all the time by her distant husband, and they're both dead now. The world is full of the ruins of all kinds of love it killed – gay love, straight love, romantic love, platonic love. How do people keep it safe at all? How do they maintain love in this place?

It hasn't been kind to Beau and me, either, in some ways. Our former "friend" – I won't even say his name here – has not said a word about either of us, but he hasn't exactly told the world, either. We have a sort of unspoken truce in place, but he has been whispering hints here and there, and they're getting back to me in the forms of confused questions and questioning glances. Soon we will have to confront some things, considering we live in a place like South Carolina, a place where politicians were calling for outlawing gay sex until a few decades ago. That day will come, and I will have to be ready.

But, another spoiler alert: love can also be kind in other ways. Oh, it can be *so* kind, actually. It can be kind in the way I wake up every morning and get to rest my hand on the back of the guy I am starting to full-fledged love, in every sense of the word, not just in a friendly sense or a platonic sense, but in a sense that makes me so happy I cannot sleep at night sometimes. It can be kind in the way I've unofficially moved into his small apartment downtown, making every day a new miracle. Yes, in some ways, the world has been kinder than kind to us…

I have never been this happy in my life – yes, we face certain obstacles, but I am drenched in sunlight all the same. I am happy to step out of bed, I am happy to take out the garbage, I am happy to go about my business all day because it means I am one minute closer to getting to see him again, getting to grab him by the jaw and kiss all of my happiness into him. Nobody knows about us yet, but thanks to Lane they will eventually – and I am absolutely fortified in the knowledge that we will get through it when it comes. I think we could get through anything.

We are still figuring out how to transition from friends to partners, yes. Sometimes I don't know the exact right thing to say, and I can feel that sometimes he doesn't know how he should touch me in a certain moment. For some reason, all this has dug up his old fears and terrors about his mom, too, and sometimes he gets anxiety nightmares that make him wake up screaming. But we are getting there, and what we are finding is blowing my world open. But he is here, and I am a poet now.

Yes, you heard me correctly – I've listened to Beau's advice, and I am putting all my thoughts into verse. I will never show a soul, though, because our light and our magic and our love – it all belongs to us. My poetry is only for him – I am his personal poet laureate. In fact, I leave my poetry notebook on our bedside table every morning so he can sink into my feelings for him whenever he wants to. And sometimes I sit there and watch him silently, just watching him enjoy my account of what it is like to love him through my own eyes. And I hope I will never have to stop. His happiness means more to me than my own happiness does now. And as long as he's good, I'm good, too. Who knows, maybe I'll publish a copy of all my poems one day – only for him, though. One copy only.

On a Friday in September, I throw my bike to the ground and run up the steps to our building. I dash up the stairs to our unit, and there he is – well, his *voice* at least, as he attempts to cook in the kitchen. His cooking attempts aren't getting any better, but I'm trying not to say anything. I will eat one million burned grilled cheese sandwiches if it means getting to be with him, and getting to avoid the future I saw in that nightmarish fever-dream. I don't care about the details anymore, because we are *living* now – living in a way I never knew to be possible. Who thought one random hookup could've led to a whole new life? Or maybe we already knew it. Maybe we *always* knew it. Maybe we just needed some cheap vodka and some bravado to help force it out of ourselves...

I reach into my pocket and play with the gift I made him this morning, just because. After his parents died, Beau had a bit of a meltdown and poured water on most of the pictures he had of them, overcome with what I guessed was anger and helplessness and confusion. So the pictures he has of them now, he can count on two hands. But last night, as I sifted through some of my old things, I found a shot that took my breath away – it was me, Beau, and Beau's mom, on a dock out in the Sea Islands somewhere. We were light-haired and tiny, laughing and yelling as his mom pulled in a tiny little fish. We looked so happy, so...pure, that I knew I was going to frame it and give it to Beau just as soon as I could. He is the biggest part of my past, and I hope to God we can be each other's futures – just in a different way. A new way. A perfect way.

In the entry hallway I think back to the younger version of me, the little boy who was different and didn't know what to do about it. The boy who was an invisible nerd until Beau arrived on my street. The boy who was alone sometimes, who would get left behind and didn't understand why. The boy who sometimes felt things for his best friend and tried to hide those things, to stamp them out like a lit cigarette on a sidewalk, because that friend happened to be a boy. That boy was so afraid, so alone. Looking back, I wish I could find that boy, that terrified version of me. I would walk up to him as he stared out at the playground or lay in his bed burying his feelings in a book, and I would tell him there was nothing wrong with him at all. In fact, I would dazzle him with the future. I would tell him that one day, a time would come when he didn't hate the "different" parts of himself at all – that one day, he would open himself to the love he felt for that friend, and that his friend would open himself, too, and that their love would light up a whole world.

I round the corner into the kitchen, where Beau leans against the sink in nothing but an apron, singing along to this awful disco-pop song. Oh, yes, I know straight where this is going tonight – but first I want to dance with him, even if his taste in music has always been hilariously awful. But from kindergarten finger paintings to teenage trampoline dreams to one shared adulthood, lived within a different kind of love – in this moment I feel without a doubt that everything has led to here.

"Stop that right now," I say into his ear by way of greeting, wrapping an arm around him and pulling him into me.

"Why, babe?" he asks into my mouth as we kiss. I squeeze him even closer and inhale the soapy scent of the guy who was my best friend, then became my lover, and is now my forever partner, hopefully...

"Because you don't ever have to sing alone again. I'm here now. You sing, I sing, remember?"

The End
For more on Seth King, please follow him on Facebook

Made in the USA
Columbia, SC
23 December 2022